THE TOR DOUBLES

Tor is proud to bring you the best in science fiction's short novels. An amazing amount of particularly fine science fiction is written at a length just too short to put in a book by itself, so we're providing them two at a time.

The Tor Doubles will be both new stories and older ones, all carefully chosen. Whichever side you start with, you will be able to turn the book over and enjoy the other side just as much.

"HOLD IT OR I'LL SHOOT!"

Speyer's cry was ignored.

Mackenzie couldn't bring himself to fire on unarmed men. He gave the youngster before him the pistol barrel in his teeth. Bloody-faced, the Esper lurched back. Mackenzie stiff-armed the one coming in from the left. The third tried to fill the doorway. Mackenzie put a foot behind his ankles and pushed. As he went down, Mackenzie kicked him in the temple, hard enough to stun, and jumped over him.

The fourth was on his back. Mackenzie writhed about to face the man. Those arms that hugged him, pinioning his gun, were bear-strong. Mackenzie put the butt of his free left hand under the fellow's nose, and pushed. The acolyte let go. Mackenzie gave him a knee in the stomach, whirled, and ran.

There was not much further commotion behind him. He looked out the open entrance, onto the square. Sunlight hurt his eyes. His breath came in painful gulps, there was a stitch in his side, yeah, he was getting old.

**Also by Poul Anderson
published by Tor Books**

Conflict
The Gods Laughed
The Guardians of Time
Hoka! (with Gordon R. Dickson)
A Midsummer Tempest
New America
Past Times
Psychotechnic League
Tales of the Flying Mountains
Time Wars

POUL ANDERSON
NO TRUCE WITH KINGS

A TOM DOHERTY ASSOCIATES BOOK
NEW YORK

NO TRUCE WITH KINGS

Copyright © 1963 by Mercury Press, Inc.

Reprinted by permission of the author and his agent, Scott Meredith Literary Agency, Inc.

A TOR Book
Published by Tom Doherty Associates, Inc.
49 West 24 Street
New York, NY 10010

Cover art by Royo

ISBN: 0-812-55958-4   Can. ISBN: 0-812-55954-1

First Tor edition: February 1989

Printed in the United States of America

0 9 8 7 6 5 4 3 2 1

"SONG, Charlie! Give's a song!"
"Yay, Charlie!"

The whole mess was drunk, and the junior officers at the far end of the table were only somewhat noisier than their seniors near the colonel. Rugs and hangings could not much muffle the racket, shouts, stamping boots, thump of fists on oak and clash of cups raised aloft, that rang from wall to stony wall. High up among shadows that hid the rafters they hung from, the regimental banners stirred in a draft, as if to join the chaos. Below, the light of bracketed lanterns and bellowing fireplace winked on trophies and weapons.

Autumn comes early on Echo Summit, and it was storming outside, wind-hoot past the watchtowers and rain-rush in the courtyards, an undertone that walked through the buildings and down all corridors, as if the story were true that the unit's dead came out of the cemetery each September Nineteenth night and tried to join the celebration but had

1

forgotten how. No one let it bother him, here or in the enlisted barracks, except maybe the hex major. The Third Division, the Catamounts, was best known as the most riotous gang in the Army of the Pacific States of America, and of its regiments the Rolling Stones who held Fort Nakamura were the wildest.

"Go on, boy! Lead off. You've got the closest thing to a voice in the whole goddamn Sierra," Colonel Mackenzie called. He loosened the collar of his black dress tunic and lounged back, legs asprawl, pipe in one hand and beaker of whiskey in the other: a thickset man with blue wrinkle-meshed eyes in a battered face, his cropped hair turned gray but his mustache still arrogantly red.

"Charlie is my darlin', my darlin', my darlin'," sang Captain Hulse. He stopped as the noise abated a little. Young Lieutenant Amadeo got up, grinned, and launched into one they well knew.

"I am a Catamountain, I guard a border pass.
And every time I venture out, the cold will freeze m—"

"Colonel, sir. Begging your pardon."

Mackenzie twisted around and looked into the face of Sergeant Irwin. The man's expression shocked him. "Yes?"

> *"I am a bloody hero, a decorated vet:*
> *The Order of the Purple Shaft, with*
> *pineapple clusters yet!"*

"Message just come in, sir. Major Speyer asks to see you right away."

Speyer, who didn't like being drunk, had volunteered for duty tonight; otherwise men drew lots for it on a holiday. Remembering the last word from San Francisco, Mackenzie grew chill.

The mess bawled forth the chorus, not noticing when the colonel knocked out his pipe and rose.

> *"The guns go boom! Hey, tiddley boom!*
> *The rockets vroom, the arrows zoom.*
> *From slug to slug is damn small room.*
> *Get me out of here and back to the good*
> *old womb!*
> *(Hey, doodle dee day!)"*

All right-thinking Catamounts maintained that they could operate better with the booze sloshing up to their eardrums than any other outfit cold sober. Mackenzie ignored the tingle in his veins; forgot it. He walked a straight line to the door, automatically taking his sidearm off the rack as he passed by. The song pursued him into the hall.

> *"For maggots in the rations, we hardly*
> *ever lack.*

3

You bite into a sandwich and the
  sandwich bites right back.
The coffee is the finest grade of
  Sacramento mud.
The ketchup's good in combat, though,
  for simulating blood.

(Cho-orus!)

The drums go bump! Ah-tumpty-tump!
The bugles make like Gabri-l's
  trump—"

Lanterns were far apart in the passage. Portraits of former commanders watched the colonel and the sergeant from eyes that were hidden in grotesque darkness. Footfalls clattered too loudly here.

"I've got an arrow in my rump.
  Right about and rearward, heroes, on
    the jump!
  (Hey, doodle dee day!)"

Mackenzie went between a pair of field-pieces flanking a stairway—they had been captured at Rock Springs during the Wyoming War, a generation ago—and upward. There was more distance between places in this keep than his legs liked at their present age. But it was old, had been added to decade by decade;

4

and it needed to be massive, chiseled and mortared from Sierra granite, for it guarded a key to the nation. More than one army had broken against its revetments, before the Nevada marches were pacified, and more young men than Mackenzie wished to think about had gone from this base to die among angry strangers.

But she's never been attacked from the west. God, or whatever you are, you can spare her that, can't you?

The command office was lonesome at this hour. The room where Sergeant Irwin had his desk lay so silent: no clerks pushing pens, no messengers going in or out, no wives making a splash of color with their dresses as they waited to see the colonel about some problem down in the Village. When he opened the door to the inner room, though, Mackenzie heard the wind shriek around the angle of the wall. Rain slashed at the black windowpane and ran down in streams which the lanterns turned molten.

"Here the colonel is, sir," Irwin said in an uneven voice. He gulped and closed the door behind Mackenzie.

Speyer stood by the commander's desk. It was a beat-up old object with little upon it: an inkwell, a letter basket, an interphone, a photograph of Nora, faded in these dozen years since her death. The major was a tall and gaunt man, hook-nosed, going bald on top. His uni-

5

form always looked unpressed, somehow. But he had the sharpest brain in the Cats, Mackenzie thought; and Christ, how could any man read as many books as Phil did! Officially he was the adjutant, in practice the chief adviser.

"Well?" Mackenzie said. The alcohol did not seem to numb him, rather make him too acutely aware of things: how the lanterns smelled hot (when would they get a big enough generator to run electric lights?), and the floor was hard under his feet, and a crack went through the plaster of the north wall, and the stove wasn't driving out much of the chill. He forced bravado, stuck thumbs in belt and rocked back on his heels. "Well, Phil, what's wrong now?"

"Wire from Frisco," Speyer said. He had been folding and unfolding a piece of paper, which he handed over.

"Huh? Why not a radio call?"

"Telegram's less likely to be intercepted. This one's in code, at that. Irwin decoded it for me."

"What the hell kind of nonsense is this?"

"Have a look, Jimbo, and you'll find out. It's for you, anyway. Direct from GHQ."

Mackenzie focused on Irwin's scrawl. The usual formalities of an order; then:

You are hereby notified that the Pacific States Senate has passed a bill of impeachment against Owen Brodsky, formerly Judge of the Pacific States of America, and deprived him of office. As of 2000 hours this date, former Vice Humphrey Fallon is Judge of the PSA in accordance with the Law of Succession. The existence of dissident elements constituting a public danger has made it necessary for Judge Fallon to put the entire nation under martial law, effective at 2100 hours this date. You are therefore issued the following instructions:

1. The above intelligence is to be held strictly confidential until an official proclamation is made. No person who has received knowledge in the course of transmitting this message shall divulge same to any other person whatsoever. Violators of this section and anyone thereby receiving information shall be placed immediately in solitary confinement to await court-martial.

2. You will sequestrate all arms and ammunition except for ten percent of available stock, and keep same under heavy guard.

3. You will keep all men in the Fort Nakamura area until you are relieved. Your relief is Colonel Simon Hollis, who will start from San Francisco tomorrow morning with one battalion. They are expected to arrive at Fort Nakamura in

five days, at which time you will surrender your command to him. Colonel Hollis will designate those officers and enlisted men who are to be replaced by members of his battalion, which will be integrated into the regiment. You will lead the men replaced back to San Francisco and report to Brigadier General Mendoza at New Fort Baker. To avoid provocations, these men will be disarmed except for officers' sidearms.

4. For your private information, Captain Thomas Danielis has been appointed senior aide to Colonel Hollis.

5. You are again reminded that the Pacific States of America are under martial law because of a national emergency. Complete loyalty to the legal government is required. Any mutinous talk must be severely punished. Anyone giving aid or comfort to the Brodsky faction is guilty of treason and will be dealt with accordingly.

Gerald O'Donnell, Gen. APSA, CINC

Thunder went off in the mountains like artillery. It was a while before Mackenzie stirred, and then merely to lay the paper on his desk. He could only summon feeling slowly, up into a hollowness that filled his skin.

"They dared," Speyer said without tone. "They really did."

"Huh?" Mackenzie swiveled eyes around to

the major's face. Speyer didn't meet that stare. He was concentrating his own gaze on his hands, which were now rolling a cigarette. But the words jerked from him, harsh and quick:

"I can guess what happened. The warhawks have been hollering for impeachment ever since Brodsky compromised the border dispute with West Canada. And Fallon, yeah, he's got ambitions of his own. But his partisans are a minority and he knows it. Electing him Vice helped soothe the warhawks some, but he'd never make Judge the regular way, because Brodsky isn't going to die of old age before Fallon does, and anyhow more than fifty percent of the Senate are sober, satisfied bossmen who don't agree that the PSA has a divine mandate to reunify the continent. I don't see how an impeachment could get through an honestly convened Senate. More likely they'd vote out Fallon."

"But a Senate had been called," Mackenzie said. The words sounded to him like someone else talking. "The newscasts told us."

"Sure. Called for yesterday 'to debate ratification of the treaty with West Canada.' But the bossmen are scattered up and down the country, each at his own Station. They have to *get* to San Francisco. A couple of arranged delays— hell, if a bridge just happened to be blown on the Boise railroad, a round dozen of Brodsky's staunchest supporters wouldn't arrive on time —so the Senate has a quorum, all right, but

9

every one of Fallon's supporters are there, and so many of the rest are missing that the warhawks have a clear majority. Then they meet on a holiday, when no cityman is paying attention. Presto, impeachment and a new Judge!" Speyer finished his cigarette and stuck it between his lips while he fumbled for a match. A muscle twitched in his jaw.

"You sure?" Mackenzie mumbled. He thought dimly that this moment was like one time he'd visited Puget City and been invited for a sail on the Guardian's yacht, and a fog had closed in. Everything was cold and blind, with nothing you could catch in your hands.

"Of course I'm not sure!" Speyer snarled. "Nobody will be sure till it's too late." The matchbox shook in his grasp.

"They, uh, they got a new Cinc too, I noticed."

"Uh-huh. They'd want to replace everybody they can't trust, as fast as possible, and De Barros was a Brodsky appointee." The match flared with a hellish *scrit*. Speyer inhaled till his cheeks collapsed. "You and me included, naturally. The regiment reduced to minimum armament so that nobody will get ideas about resistance when the new colonel arrives. You'll note he's coming with a battalion at his heels just the same, just in case. Otherwise he could take a plane and be here tomorrow."

"Why not a train?" Mackenzie caught a whiff of smoke and felt for his pipe. The bowl was hot in his tunic pocket.

"Probably all rolling stock has to head north. Get troops among the bossmen there to forestall a revolt. The valleys are safe enough, peaceful ranchers and Esper colonies. None of them'll potshot Fallonite soldiers marching to garrison Echo and Donner outposts." A dreadful scorn weighted Speyer's words.

"What are we going to do?"

"I assume Fallon's take-over followed legal forms; that there was a quorum," Speyer said. "Nobody will ever agree whether it was really Constitutional . . . I've been reading this damned message over and over since Irwin decoded it. There's a lot between the lines. I think Brodsky's at large, for instance. If he were under arrest this would've said as much, and there'd have been less worry about rebellion. Maybe some of his household troops smuggled him away in time. He'll be hunted like a jackrabbit, of course."

Mackenzie took out his pipe but forgot he had done so. "Tom's coming with our replacements," he said thinly.

"Yeah. Your son-in-law. That was a smart touch, wasn't it? A kind of hostage for your good behavior, but also a back-hand promise that you and yours won't suffer if you report in as ordered. Tom's a good kid. He'll stand by his own."

"This is his regiment too," Mackenzie said. He squared his shoulders. "He wanted to fight West Canada, sure. Young and . . . and a lot of Pacificans did get killed in the Idaho Panhandle during the skirmishes. Women and kids among 'em."

"Well," Speyer said, "you're the colonel, Jimbo. What should we do?"

"Oh, Jesus, I don't know. I'm nothing but a soldier." The pipestem broke in Mackenzie's fingers. "But we're not some bossman's personal militia here. We swore to support the Constitution."

"*I* can't see where Brodsky's yielding some of our claims in Idaho is grounds for impeachment. I think he was right."

"Well—"

"A *coup d'etat* by any other name would stink as bad. You may not be much of a student of current events, Jimbo, but you know as well as I do what Fallon's Judgeship will mean. War with West Canada is almost the least of it. Fallon also stands for a strong central government. He'll find ways to grind down the old bossman families. A lot of their heads and scions will die in the front lines; that stunt goes back to David and Uriah. Others will be accused of collusion with the Brodsky people —not altogether falsely—and impoverished by fines. Esper communities will get nice big land grants, so their economic competition can bankrupt still other estates. Later wars will keep bossmen away for years at a time, unable to supervise their own affairs, which will therefore go to the devil. And thus we march toward the glorious goal of Reunification."

"If Esper Central favors him, what can we do? I've heard enough about psi blasts. I can't ask my men to face them."

"You could ask your men to face the Hellbomb itself, Jimbo, and they would. A Mackenzie has commanded the Rolling Stones for over fifty years."

"Yes. I thought Tom, someday—"

"We've watched this brewing for a long time. Remember the talk we had about it last week?"

"Uh-huh."

"I might also remind you that the Constitution was written explicitly 'to confirm the separate regions in their ancient liberties.'"

"Let me alone!" Mackenzie shouted. "I don't know what's right or wrong, I tell you! Let me alone!"

Speyer fell silent, watching him through a screen of foul smoke. Mackenzie walked back and forth a while, boots slamming the floor like drumbeats. Finally he threw the broken pipe across the room so it shattered.

"Okay." He must ram each word past the tension in his throat. "Irwin's a good man who can keep his lip buttoned. Send him out to cut the telegraph line a few miles downhill. Make it look as if the storm did it. The wire breaks often enough, heaven knows. Officially, then, we never got GHQ's message. That gives us a few days to contact Sierra Command HQ. I won't go against General Cruikshank . . . but I'm pretty sure which way he'll go if he sees a chance. Tomorrow we prepare for action. It'll be no trick to throw back Hollis' battalion, and they'll need a while to bring some real strength against us. Before then the first snow should be along, and we'll be shut off for the winter. Only we can use skis and snowshoes, ourselves, to keep in touch with the other units and organize something. By spring— we'll see what happens."

"Thanks, Jimbo." The wind almost drowned Speyer's words.

"I'd . . . I'd better go tell Laura."

"Yeah." Speyer squeezed Mackenzie's shoulder. There were tears in the major's eyes.

Mackenzie went out with parade-ground steps, ignoring Irwin: down the hall, down a stairway at its other end, past guarded doors where he returned salutes without really noticing, and so to his own quarters in the south wing.

His daughter had gone to sleep already. He took a lantern off its hook in his bleak little parlor, and entered her room. She had come back here while her husband was in San Francisco.

For a moment Mackenzie couldn't quite remember why he had sent Tom there. He passed a hand over his stubbly scalp, as if to squeeze something out . . . oh, yes, ostensibly to arrange for a new issue of uniforms; actually to get the boy out of the way until the political crisis had blown over. Tom was too honest for his own good, an admirer of Fallon and the Esper movement. His outspokenness had led to friction with his brother officers. They were mostly of bossman stock or from well-to-do protectee families. The existing social order had been good to them. But Tom Danielis began as a fisher lad in a poverty-stricken village on the Mendocino coast. In spare moments he'd learned the three R's from a local Esper; once literate, he joined the Army and earned a commission by sheer guts and brains. He had never forgotten that the Espers helped the poor and that Fallon promised to help the Espers . . . Then, too, battle, glory, Reunification, Federal Democracy, those were heady dreams when you were young.

Laura's room was little changed since she left it to get married last year. And she had only been seventeen then. Objects survived which had belonged to a small person with pigtails and starched frocks—a teddy bear loved to shapelessness, a doll house her father had built, her mother's picture drawn by a corporal who stopped a bullet at Salt Lake. Oh, God, how much she had come to look like her mother.

Dark hair streamed over a pillow turned gold by the light. Mackenzie shook her as gently as he was able. She awoke instantly, and he saw the terror within her.

"Dad! Anything about Tom?"

"He's okay." Mackenzie set the lantern on the floor and himself on the edge of the bed. Her fingers were cold where they caught at his hand.

"He isn't," she said. "I know you too well."

"He's not been hurt yet. I hope he won't be."

Mackenzie braced himself. Because she was a soldier's daughter, he told her the truth in a few words; but he was not strong enough to look at her while he did. When he had finished, he sat dully listening to the rain.

"You're going to revolt," she whispered.

"I'm going to consult with SCHQ and follow my commanding officer's orders," Mackenzie said.

"You know what they'll be . . . once he knows you'll back him."

Mackenzie shrugged. His head had begun to ache. Hangover started already? He'd need a good deal more booze before he could sleep tonight. No, no time for sleep—yes, there would be. Tomorrow would do to assemble the regiment in the courtyard and address them from the breech of Black Hepzibah, as a Mackenzie of the Rolling Stones always addressed his men, and—. He found himself ludicrously recalling a day when he and Nora and this girl here had gone rowing on Lake Tahoe. The water was the color of Nora's eyes, green and blue and with sunlight flimmering across the surface, but so clear you could see the rocks on the bottom; and Laura's own little bottom had stuck straight in the air as she trailed her hands astern.

She sat thinking for a space before saying flatly: "I suppose you can't be talked out of it." He shook his head. "Well, can I leave tomorrow early, then?"

"Yes. I'll get you a coach."

"T-t-to hell with that. I'm better in the saddle than you are."

"Okay. A couple of men to escort you, though." Mackenzie drew a long breath. "Maybe you can persuade Tom—"

"No. I can't. Please don't ask me to, Dad."

He gave her the last gift he could: "I wouldn't want you to stay. That'd be shirking your own duty. Tell Tom I still think he's the right man for you. Goodnight, duck." It came out too fast, but he dared not delay. When she began to cry he must unfold her arms from his neck and depart the room.

"But I had not expected so much killing!"

"Nor I . . . at this stage of things. There will be more yet, I am afraid, before the immediate purpose is achieved."

"You told me—"

"I told you our hopes, Mwyr. You know as well as I that the Great Science is only exact on the broadest scale of history. Individual events are subject to statistical fluctuation."

17

"That is an easy way, is it not, to describe sentient beings dying in the mud?"

"You are new here. Theory is one thing, adjustment to practical necessities is another. Do you think it does not hurt me to see that happen which I myself have helped plan?"

"Oh, I know, I know. Which makes it easier to live with my guilt."

"To live with your responsibilities, you mean."

"Your phrase."

"No, this is not semantic trickery. The distinction is real. You have read reports and seen films, but I was here with the first expedition. And here I have been for more than two centuries. Their agony is no abstraction to me."

"But it was different when we first discovered them. The aftermath of their nuclear wars was still so horribly present. That was when they needed us—the poor starveling anarchs—and we, we did nothing but observe."

"Now you are hysterical. Could we come in blindly, ignorant of every last fact about them, and expect to be anything but one more disruptive element? An element whose effects we ourselves would not have been able to predict. That would have been criminal indeed, like a surgeon who started to operate as soon as he met the patient, *without so much as taking a case history. We had to let them go their own way while we studied in secret. You have no idea how desperately hard we worked to gain information and understanding. That work goes on. It was only seventy years ago that we felt enough assurance to introduce the first new factor into this one selected society. As we continue to learn more, the plan will be adjusted. It may take us a thousand years to complete our mission."*

"But meanwhile they have pulled themselves back out of the wreckage. They are finding their own answers to their problems. What right have we to—"

"I begin to wonder, Mwyr, what right you have to claim even the title of apprentice psychodynamician. Consider what their 'answers' actually amount to. Most of the planet is still in a state of barbarism. This continent has come farthest toward recovery, because of having the widest distribution of technical skills and equipment before the destruction. But what social structure has evolved? A jumble of quarrelsome successor states. A feudalism where the balance of political, military, and economic power lies with a landed aristocracy, of all archaic things. A score of languages and subcultures developing along their own incompatible lines. A blind technology worship inherited from the an-

cestral society that, unchecked, will lead them in the end back to a machine civilization as demoniac as the one that tore itself apart three centuries ago. Are you distressed that a few hundred men have been killed because our agents promoted a revolution which did not come off quite so smoothly as we hoped? Well, you have the word of the Great Science itself that, without our guidance, the totaled misery of this race through the next five thousand years would outweigh by three orders of magnitude whatever pain we are forced to inflict."

"—Yes. Of course. I realize I am being emotional. It is difficult not to be at first, I suppose."

"You should be thankful that your initial exposure to the hard necessities of the plan was so mild. There is worse to come."

"So I have been told."

"In abstract terms. But consider the reality. A government ambitious to restore the old nation will act aggressively, thus embroiling itself in prolonged wars with powerful neighbors. Both directly and indirectly, through the operation of economic factors they are too naive to control, the aristocrats and freeholders will be eroded away by those wars. Anomic democracy will replace their system, first dominated by a corrupt capitalism and later by sheer force of whoever holds the *central government. But there will be no place for the vast displaced proletariat, the one-time landowners and the foreigners incorporated by conquest. They will offer fertile soil to any demagogue. The empire will undergo endless upheaval, civil strife, depotism, decay, and outside invasion. Oh, we will have much to answer for before we are done!"*

"Do you think . . . when we see the final result . . . will the blood wash off us?"

"No. We pay the heaviest price of all."

Spring in the high Sierra is cold, wet, snow-banks melting away from forest floor and giant rocks, rivers in spate until their canyons clang, a breeze ruffling puddles in the road. The first green breath across the aspen seems infinitely tender against pine and spruce, which gloom into a brilliant sky. A raven swoops low, gruk, gruk, look out for that damn hawk! But then you cross timber line and the world becomes tumbled blue-gray immensity, with the sun ablaze on what snows remain and the wind sounding hollow in your ears.

Captain Thomas Danielis, Field Artillery, Loyalist Army of the Pacific States, turned his horse aside. He was a dark young man, slender and snub-nosed. Behind him a squad slipped and cursed, dripping mud from feet to helmets, trying to get a gun carrier unstuck. Its alcohol motor was too feeble to do more than spin the wheels. The infantry squelched on past, stoop-shouldered, worn down by altitude and a wet bivouac and pounds of mire on each boot. Their line snaked from around a prowlike crag, up the twisted road and over the ridge ahead. A gust brought the smell of sweat to Danielis.

But they were good joes, he thought. Dirty, dogged, they did their profane best. His own company, at least, was going to get hot food tonight, if he had to cook the quartermaster sergeant.

The horse's hoofs banged on a block of ancient concrete jutting from the muck. If this had been the old days . . . but wishes weren't bullets. Beyond this part of the range lay lands mostly desert, claimed by the Saints, who were no longer a menace but with whom there was scant commerce. So the mountain highways had never been considered worth repaving, and the railroad ended at Hangtown. Therefore the expeditionary force to the Tahoe area must slog through unpeopled forests and icy uplands, God help the poor bastards.

God help them in Nakamura, too, Danielis thought. His mouth drew taut, he slapped his hands together and spurred the horse with needless violence. Sparks shot from iron shoes as the beast clattered off the road toward the highest point of the ridge. The man's saber banged his leg.

Reining in, he unlimbered his field glasses. From here he could look across a jumbled sweep of mountainscape, where cloud shadows sailed over cliffs and boulders, down into the gloom of a canyon and across to the other side. A few tufts of grass thrust out beneath him, mummy brown, and a marmot wakened early from winter sleep whistled somewhere in the stone confusion. He still couldn't see the castle. Nor had he expected to, as yet. He knew this country . . . how well he did!

There might be a glimpse of hostile activity, though. It had been eerie to march this far with no sign of the enemy, of anyone else whatsoever; to send out patrols in search of rebel units that could not be found; to ride with shoulder muscles tense against the sniper's arrow that never came. Old Jimbo Mackenzie was not one to sit passive behind walls, and the Rolling Stones had not been given their nickname in jest.

If Jimbo is alive. How do I know he is? That buzzard yonder may be the very one which hacked out his eyes.

Danielis bit his lip and made himself look steadily through the glasses. Don't think about Mackenzie, how he outroared and outdrank and outlaughed you and you never minded, how he sat knotting his brows over the chessboard where you could mop him up ten times out of ten and *he* never cared, how proud and happy he stood at the wedding. . . . Nor think about Laura, who tried to keep you from knowing how often she wept at night, who

23

now bore a grandchild beneath her heart and woke alone in the San Francisco house from the evil dreams of pregnancy. Every one of those dogfaces plodding toward the castle which has killed every army ever sent against it—every one of them has somebody at home and hell rejoices at how many have somebody on the rebel side. Better look for hostile spoor and let it go at that.

Wait! Danielis stiffened. A rider— He focused. *One of our own.* Fallon's army added a blue band to the uniform. *Returning scout.* A tingle went along his spine. He decided to hear the report firsthand. But the fellow was still a mile off, perforce riding slowly over the hugger-mugger terrain. There was no hurry about intercepting him. Danielis continued to survey the land.

A reconnaissance plane appeared, an ungainly dragonfly with sunlight flashing off a propeller head. Its drone bumbled among rock walls, where echoes threw the noise back and forth. Doubtless an auxiliary to the scouts, employing two-way radio communication. Later the plane would work as a spotter for artillery. There was no use making a bomber of it; Fort Nakamura was proof against anything that today's puny aircraft could drop, and might well shoot the thing down.

A shoe scraped behind Danielis. Horse and man whirled as one. His pistol jumped into his hand.

It lowered. "Oh. Excuse me, Philosopher."

The man in the blue robe nodded. A smile softened his stern face. He must be around sixty years old, hair white and skin lined, but he walked these heights like a wild goat. The Yang and Yin symbol burned gold on his breast.

"You're needlessly on edge, son," he said. A trace of Texas accent stretched out his words. The Espers obeyed the laws wherever they lived, but acknowledged no country their own: nothing less than mankind, perhaps ultimately all life through the space-time universe. Nevertheless, the Pacific States had gained enormously in prestige and influence when the Order's unenterable Central was established in San Francisco at the time when the city was being rebuilt in earnest. There had been no objection—on the contrary—to the Grand Seeker's desire that Philosopher Woodworth accompany the expedition as an observer. Not even from the chaplains; the churches had finally gotten it straight that the Esper teachings were neutral with respect to religion.

Danielis managed a grin. "Can you blame me?"

"No blame. But advice. Your attitude isn't useful. Does nothin' but wear out. You've been fightin' a battle for weeks before it began."

Danielis remembered the apostle who had visited his home in San Francisco—by invitation, in the hope that Laura might learn some peace. His simile had been still homelier: "You only need to wash one dish at a time." The memory brought a smart to Danielis' eyes, so that he said roughly:

"I might relax if you'd use your powers to tell me what's waiting for us."

"I'm no adept, son. Too much in the material world, I'm afraid. Somebody's got to do the practical work of the Order, and someday I'll get the chance to retire and explore the frontier inside me. But you need to start early, and stick to it a lifetime, to develop your full powers." Woodworth looked across the peaks, seemed almost to merge himself with their loneliness.

Danielis hesitated to break into the meditation. He wondered what practical purpose the Philosopher was serving on this trip. To bring back a report, more accurate than untrained senses and undisciplined emotions could prepare? Yes, that must be it. The Espers might yet decide to take a hand in this war. However reluctantly, Central had allowed the awesome psi powers to be released now and again, when the Order was seriously threatened; and Judge Fallon was a better friend to them than Brodsky or the earlier Senate of Bossmen and House of People's Deputies had been.

The horse stamped and blew out its breath in a snort. Woodworth glanced back at the rider. "If you ask me, though," he said, "I don't reckon you'll find much doin' around here. I was in the Rangers myself, back home, before I saw the Way. This country feels empty."

"If we could know!" Danielis exploded. "They've had the whole winter to do what they liked in the mountains, while the snow kept us out. What scouts we could get in reported a beehive—as late as two weeks ago. What have they planned?"

Woodworth made no reply.

It flooded from Danielis, he couldn't stop, he had to cover the recollection of Laura bidding him good-by on his second expedition against her father, six months after the first one came home in bloody fragments:

"If we had the resources! A few wretched little railroads and motor cars; a handful of aircraft; most of our supply trains drawn by mules—what kind of mobility does that give us? And what really drives me crazy . . . we know how to make what they had in the old days. We've got the books, the information. More, maybe, than the ancestors. I've watched the electrosmith at Fort Nakamura turn out transistor units with enough bandwidth to carry television, no bigger than my fist. I've seen the scientific journals, the research labs, biology, chemistry, astronomy, mathematics. And all useless!"

"Not so," Woodworth answered mildly.

"Like my own Order, the community of scholarship's becomin' supranational. Printin' presses, radiophones, telescribes—"

"I say useless. Useless to stop men killing each other because there's no authority strong enough to make them behave. Useless to take a farmer's hands off a horse-drawn plow and put them on the wheel of a tractor. We've got the knowledge, but we can't apply it."

"You do apply it, son, where too much power and industrial plant isn't required. Remember, the world's a lot poorer in natural resources than it was before the Hellbombs. I've seen the Black Lands myself, where the firestorm passed over the Texas oilfields." Woodworth's serenity cracked a little. He turned his eyes back to the peaks.

"There's oil elsewhere," Danielis insisted. "And coal, iron, uranium, everything we need. But the world hasn't got the organization to get at it. Not in any quantity. So we fill the Central Valley with crops that'll yield alcohol, to keep a few motors turning; and we import a dribble of other stuff along an unbelievably inefficient chain of middlemen; and most of it's eaten by the armies." He jerked his head toward that part of the sky which the handmade airplane had crossed. "That's one reason we've got to have Reunification. So we can rebuild."

"And the other?" Woodworth asked softly.

"Democracy—universal suffrage—" Danielis swallowed. "And so fathers and sons won't have to fight each other again."

"Those are better reasons," Woodworth said. "Good enough for the Espers to support. But as for that machinery you want—" He shook his head. "No, you're wrong there. That's no way for men to live."

"Maybe not," Danielis said. "Though my own father wouldn't have been crippled by overwork if he'd had some machines to help him . . . Oh, I don't know. First things first. Let's get this war over with and argue later." He remembered the scout, now gone from view. "Pardon me, Philosopher, I've got an errand."

The Esper raised his hand in token of peace. Danielis cantered off.

Splashing along the roadside, he saw the man he wanted, halted by Major Jacobsen. The latter, who must have sent him out, sat mounted near the infantry line. The scout was a Klamath Indian, stocky in buckskins, a bow on his shoulder. Arrows were favored over guns by many of the men from the northern districts: cheaper than bullets, no noise, less range but as much firepower as a bolt-action rifle. In the bad old days before the Pacific States had formed their union, archers along forest trails had saved many a town from conquest; they still helped keep that union loose.

"Ah, Captain Danielis," Jacobsen hailed.

"You're just in time. Lieutenant Smith was about to report what his detachment found out."

"And the plane," said Smith imperturbably. "What the pilot told us he'd seen from the air gave us the guts to go there and check for ourselves."

"Well?"

"Nobody around."

"What?"

"Fort's been evacuated. So's the settlement. Not a soul."

"But—what—" Jacobsen collected himself. "Go on."

"We studied the signs as best's we could. Looks like noncombatants left some time ago. By sledge and ski, I'd guess, maybe north to some strong point. I suppose the men shifted their own stuff at the same time, gradual-like, what they couldn't carry with 'em at the last. Because the regiment and its support units, even field artillery, pulled out just three-four days ago. Ground's all tore up. They headed downslope, sort of west by northwest, far's we could tell from what we saw."

Jacobsen choked. "Where are they bound?"

A flaw of wind struck Danielis in the face and ruffled the horses' manes. At his back he heard the slow plop and squish of boots, groan of wheels, chuff of motors, rattle of wood and metal, yells and whipcracks of muleskinners.

But it seemed very remote. A map grew before him, blotting out the world.

The Loyalist Army had had savage fighting the whole winter, from the Trinity Alps to Puget Sound—for Brodsky had managed to reach Mount Rainier, whose lord had furnished broadcasting facilities, and Rainier was too well fortified to take at once. The bossmen and the autonomous tribes rose in arms, persuaded that a usurper threatened their damned little local privileges. Their protectees fought beside them, if only because no rustic had been taught any higher loyalty than to his patron. West Canada, fearful of what Fallon might do when he got the chance, lent the rebels aid that was scarcely even clandestine.

Nonetheless, the national army was stronger: more materiel, better organization, above everything an ideal of the future. Cinc O'Donnell had outlined a strategy—concentrate the loyal forces at a few points, overwhelm resistance, restore order and establish bases in the region, then proceed to the next place—which worked. The government now controlled the entire coast, with naval units to keep an eye on the Canadians in Vancouver and guard the important Hawaii trade routes; the northern half of Washington almost to the Idaho line; the Columbia Valley; central California as far north as Redding. The remaining rebellious Stations and towns were isolated from each other in mountains, forests, deserts. Bossdom after bossdom fell as the loyalists pressed on, defeating the enemy in detail, cutting him off from supplies and hope. The only real worry had been Cruikshank's Sierra Command, an army in its own right rather than a levy of yokels and citymen, big and tough and expertly led. This expedition against Fort Nakamura was only a small part of what had looked like a difficult campaign.

But now the Rolling Stones had pulled out. Offered no fight whatsoever. Which meant that their brother Catamounts must also have evacuated. You don't give up one anchor of a line you intend to hold. So?

"Down into the valleys," Danielis said; and there sounded in his ears, crazily, the voice of Laura as she used to sing. *Down in the valley, valley so low.*

"Judas!" the major exclaimed. Even the Indian grunted as if he had taken a belly blow. "No, they couldn't. We'd have known."

Hang your head over, hear the wind blow. It hooted across cold rocks.

"There are plenty of forest trails," Danielis said. "Infantry and cavalry could use them, if they're accustomed to such country. And the Cats are. Vehicles, wagons, big guns, that's slower and harder. But they only need to outflank us, then they can get back onto Forty and Fifty—and cut us to pieces if we attempt pursuit. I'm afraid they've got us boxed."

"The eastern slope—" said Jacobsen helplessly.

"What for? Want to occupy a lot of sagebrush? No, we're trapped here till they deploy in the flatlands." Daniels closed a hand on his saddlehorn so that the knuckles went bloodless. "I miss my guess if this isn't Colonel Mackenzie's idea. It's his style, for sure."

"But then they're between us and Frisco! With damn near our whole strength in the north—"

Between me and Laura, Danielis thought.

He said aloud: "I suggest, Major, we get hold of the C.O. at once. And then we better get on the radio." From some well he drew the power to raise his head. The wind lashed his eyes. "This needn't be a disaster. They'll be easier to beat out in the open, actually, once we come to grips."

Roses love sunshine, violets love dew,
Angels in heaven know I love you.

The rains which fill the winter of the California lowlands were about ended. Northward along a highway whose pavement clopped under hoofs, Mackenzie rode through a tremendous greenness. Eucalyptus and live oak, flanking the road, exploded with new leaves. Beyond them on either side stretched a checkerboard of fields and vineyards, intricately hued, until the distant hills on the right and the higher, nearer ones on the left made walls. The freeholder houses that had been scattered across the land a ways back were no longer to be seen. This end of the Napa Valley belonged to the Esper community at St. Helena. Clouds banked like white mountains over the western ridge. The breeze bore to Mackenzie a smell of growth and turned earth.

Behind him it rumbled with men. The Rolling Stones were on the move. The regiment proper kept to the highway, three thousand boots slamming down at once with an earthquake noise, and so did the guns and wagons. There was no immediate danger of attack. But the cavalrymen attached to the force must needs spread out. The sun flashed off their helmets and lance heads.

Mackenzie's attention was directed forward. Amber walls and red tile roofs could be seen among plum trees that were a surf of pink and white blossoms. The community was big, several thousand people. The muscles tightened in his abdomen. "Think we can trust them?" he asked, not for the first time. "We've only got a radio agreement to a parley."

Speyer, riding beside him, nodded. "I expect they'll be honest. Particularly with our boys right outside. Espers believe in nonviolence anyway."

"Yeah, but if it did come to fighting—I know there aren't very many adepts so far. The

Order hasn't been around long enough for that. But when you get this many Espers together, there's bound to be a few who've gotten somewhere with their damned psionics. I don't want my men blasted, or lifted in the air and dropped, or any such nasty thing."

Speyer threw him a sidelong glance. "Are you scared of them, Jimbo?" he murmured.

"Hell, no!" Mackenzie wondered if he was a liar or not. "But I don't like 'em."

"They do a lot of good. Among the poor, especially."

"Sure, sure. Though any decent bossman looks after his own protectees, and we've got things like churches and hospices as well. I don't see where just being charitable—and they can afford it, with the profits they make on their holdings—I don't see where that gives any right to raise the orphans and pauper kids they take in, the way they do: so's to make the poor tykes unfit for life anywhere outside."

"The object of that, as you well know, is to orient them toward the so-called interior frontier. Which American civilization as a whole is not much interested in. Frankly, quite apart from the remarkable powers some Espers have developed, I often envy them."

"You, Phil?" Mackenzie goggled at his friend.

The lines drew deep in Speyer's face. "This

winter I've helped shoot a lot of my fellow countrymen," he said low. "My mother and wife and kids are crowded with the rest of the Village in the Mount Lassen fort, and when we said good-by we knew it was quite possibly permanent. And in the past I've helped shoot a lot of other men who never did me any personal harm." He sighed. "I've often wondered what it's like to know peace, inside as well as outside."

Mackenzie sent Laura and Tom out of his head.

"Of course," Speyer went on, "the fundamental reason you—and I, for that matter—distrust the Espers is that they do represent something alien to us. Something that may eventually choke out the whole concept of life that we grew up with. You know, a couple of weeks back in Sacramento I dropped in at the University research lab to see what was going on. Incredible! The ordinary soldier would swear it was witchwork. It was certainly more weird than . . . than simply reading minds or moving objects by thinking at them. But to you or me it's a shiny new marvel. We'll wallow in it.

"Now why's that? Because the lab is scientific. Those men work with chemicals, electronics, subviral particles. That fits into the educated American's world-view. But the mystic unity of creation . . . no, not our cup of tea. The only way we can hope to achieve

Oneness is to renounce everything we've ever believed in. At your age or mine, Jimbo, a man is seldom ready to tear down his whole life and start from scratch."

"Maybe so." Mackenzie lost interest. The settlement was quite near now.

He turned around to Captain Hulse, riding a few paces behind. "Here we go," he said. "Give my compliments to Lieutenant Colonel Yamaguchi and tell him he's in charge till we get back. If anything seems suspicious, he's to act at his own discretion."

"Yes, sir." Hulse saluted and wheeled smartly about. There had been no practical need for Mackenzie to repeat what had long been agreed on; but he knew the value of ritual. He clicked his big sorrel gelding into a trot. At his back he heard bugles sound orders and sergeants howl at their platoons.

Speyer kept pace. Mackenzie had insisted on bringing an extra man to the discussion. His own wits were probably no match for a high-level Esper, but Phil's might be.

Not that there's any question of diplomacy or whatever. I hope. To ease himself, he concentrated on what was real and present—hoofbeats, the rise and fall of the saddle beneath him, the horse's muscles rippling between his thighs, the creak and jingle of his saber belt, the clean odor of the animal—and suddenly remembered this was the sort of trick the Espers recommended.

None of their communities was walled, as most towns and every bossman's Station was. The officers turned off the highway and went down a street between colonnaded buildings. Side streets ran off in both directions. The settlement covered no great area, though, being composed of groups that lived together, sodalities or superfamilies or whatever you wanted to call them. Some hostility toward the Order and a great many dirty jokes stemmed from that practice. But Speyer, who should know, said there was no more sexual swapping around than in the outside world. The idea was simply to get away from possessiveness, thee versus me, and to raise children as part of a whole rather than an insular clan.

The kids were out, staring round-eyed from the porticoes, hundreds of them. They looked healthy and, underneath a natural fear of the invaders, happy enough. But pretty solemn, Mackenzie thought; and all in the same blue garb. Adults stood among them, expressionless. Everybody had come in from the fields as the regiment neared. The silence was like barricades. Mackenzie felt sweat begin to trickle down his ribs. When he emerged on the central square, he let out his breath in a near gasp.

A fountain, the basin carved into a lotus, tinkled in the middle of the plaza. Flowering trees stood around it. The square was defined on three sides by massive buildings that must be for storage. On the fourth side rose a smaller temple-like structure with a graceful cupola, obviously headquarters and meeting house. On its lowest step were ranked half a dozen blue-robed men, five of them husky youths. The sixth was middle-aged, the Yang and Yin on his breast. His features, ordinary in themselves, held an implacable calm.

Mackenzie and Speyer drew rein. The colonel flipped a soft salute. "Philosopher Gaines? I'm Mackenzie, here's Major Speyer." He swore at himself for being so awkward about it and wondered what to do with his hands. The young fellows he understood, more or less; they watched him with badly concealed hostility. But he had some trouble meeting Gaines' eyes.

The settlement leader inclined his head. "Welcome, gentlemen. Won't you come in?"

Mackenzie dismounted, hitched his horse to a post and removed his helmet. His worn reddish-brown uniform felt shabbier yet in these surroundings. "Thanks. Uh, I'll have to make this quick."

"To be sure. Follow me, please."

Stiff-backed, the young men trailed after their elders, through an entry chamber and down a short hall. Speyer looked around at the mosaics. "Why, this is lovely," he murmured.

"Thank you," said Gaines. "Here's my office." He opened a door of superbly grained walnut and gestured the visitors through.

When he closed it behind himself, the acolytes waited outside.

The room was austere, whitewashed walls enclosing little more than a desk, a shelf of books, and some backless chairs. A window opened on a garden. Gaines sat down. Mackenzie and Speyer followed suit, uncomfortable on this furniture.

"We'd better get right to business," the colonel blurted.

Gaines said nothing. At last Mackenzie must plow ahead:

"Here's the situation. Our force is to occupy Calistoga, with detachments on either side of the hills. That way we'll control both the Napa Valley and the Valley of the Moon . . . from the northern ends, at least. The best place to station our eastern wing is here. We plan to establish a fortified camp in the field yonder. I'm sorry about the damage to your crops, but you'll be compensated once the proper government has been restored. And food, medicine—you understand this army has to requisition such items, but we won't let anybody suffer undue hardship and we'll give receipts. Uh, as a precaution we'll need to quarter a few men in this community, to sort of keep an eye on things. They'll interfere as little as possible. Okay?"

"The charter of the Order guarantees exemption from military requirements," Gaines answered evenly. "In fact, no armed man is supposed to cross the boundary of any land held by an Esper settlement. I cannot be party to a violation of the law, Colonel."

"If you want to split legal hairs, Philosopher," Speyer said, "then I'll remind you that both Fallon and Judge Brodsky have declared martial law. Ordinary rules are suspended."

Gaines smiled. "Since only one government can be legitimate," he said, "the proclamations of the other are necessarily null and void. To a disinterested observer, it would appear that Judge Fallon's title is the stronger, especially when his side controls a large continuous area rather than some scattered bossdoms."

"Not any more, it doesn't," Mackenzie snapped.

Speyer gestured him back. "Perhaps you haven't followed the developments of the last few weeks, Philosopher," he said. "Allow me to recapitulate. The Sierra Command stole a march on the Fallonites and came down out of the mountains. There was almost nothing left in the middle part of California to oppose us, so we took over rapidly. By occupying Sacramento, we control river and rail traffic. Our bases extend south below Bakersfield, with Yosemite and King's Canyon not far away to provide sites for extremely strong positions. When we've consolidated this northern end of our gains, the Fallonite forces around Redding will be trapped between us and the powerful bossmen who still hold out in the Trinity,

Shasta, and Lassen regions. The very fact of
our being here has forced the enemy to evacu-
ate the Columbia Valley, so that San Francisco
may be defended. It's an open question which
side today has the last word in the larger
territory."

"What about the army that went into the
Sierra against you?" Gaines inquired shrewd-
ly. "Have you contained them?"

Mackenzie scowled. "No. That's no secret.
They got out through the Mother Lode coun-
try and went around us. They're down in Los
Angeles and San Diego now."

"A formidable host. Do you expect to stand
them off indefinitely?"

"We're going to make a hell of a good try,"
Mackenzie said. "Where we are, we've got the
advantage of interior communications. And
most of the freeholders are glad to slip us word
about whatever they observe. We can concentrate at any point the enemy starts to attack."

"Pity that this rich land must also be torn
apart by war."

"Yeah. Isn't it?"

"Our strategic objective is obvious enough,"
Speyer said. "We have cut enemy communications across the middle, except by sea, which is
not very satisfactory for troops operating far
inland. We deny him access to a good part of
his food and manufactured supplies, and most
especially to the bulk of his fuel alcohol. The
backbone of our own side is the bossdoms,

which are almost self-contained economic and social units. Before long they'll be in better shape than the rootless army they face. I think Judge Brodsky will be back in San Francisco before fall."

"If your plans succeed," Gaines said.

"That's our worry," Mackenzie leaned forward, one fist doubled on his knee. "Okay, Philosopher. I know you'd rather see Fallon come out on top, but I expect you've got more sense than to sign up in a lost cause. Will you cooperate with us?"

"The Order takes no part in political affairs, Colonel, except when its own existence is endangered."

"Oh, pipe down. By 'cooperate' I don't mean anything but keeping out from under our feet."

"I am afraid that would still count as cooperation. We cannot have military establishments on our lands."

Mackenzie stared at Gaines' face, which had set into granite lines, and wondered if he had heard aright. "Are you ordering us off?" a stranger asked with his voice.

"Yes," the Philosopher said.

"With our artillery zeroed in on your town?"

"Would you really shell women and children, Colonel?"

O Nora—"We don't need to. Our men can walk right in."

"Against psi blasts? I beg you not to have those poor boys destroyed." Gaines paused, then: "I might also point out that by losing your regiment you imperil your whole cause. You are free to march around our holdings and proceed to Calistoga."

Leaving a Fallonite nest at my back, spang across my communications southward. The teeth grated together in Mackenzie's mouth.

Gaines rose. "The discussion is at an end, gentlemen," he said. "You have one hour to get off our lands."

Mackenzie and Speyer stood up too. "We're not done yet," the major said. Sweat studded his forehead and the long nose. "I want to make some further explanations."

Gaines crossed the room and opened the door. "Show these gentlemen out," he said to the five acolytes.

"No, by God!" Mackenzie shouted. He clapped a hand to his sidearm.

"Inform the adepts," Gaines said.

One of the young men turned. Mackenzie heard the slap-slap of his sandals, running down the hall. Gaines nodded. "I think you had better go," he said.

Speyer grew rigid. His eyes shut. They flew open and he breathed, *"Inform* the adepts?"

Mackenzie saw the stiffness break in Gaines' countenance. There was no time for more than a second's bewilderment. His body acted for him. The gun clanked from his holster simultaneously with Speyer's.

"Get that messenger, Jimbo," the major rapped. "I'll keep these birds covered."

As he plunged forward, Mackenzie found himself worrying about the regimental honor. Was it right to open hostilities when you had come on a parley? But Gaines had cut the talk off himself—

"Stop him!" Gaines yelled.

The four remaining acolytes sprang into motion. Two of them barred the doorway, the other two moved in on either side. "Hold it or I'll shoot!" Speyer cried, and was ignored.

Mackenzie couldn't bring himself to fire on unarmed men. He gave the youngster before him the pistol barrel in his teeth. Bloody-faced, the Esper lurched back. Mackenzie stiff-armed the one coming in from the left. The third tried to fill the doorway. Mackenzie put a foot behind his ankles and pushed. As he went down, Mackenzie kicked him in the temple, hard enough to stun, and jumped over him.

The fourth was on his back. Mackenzie writhed about to face the man. Those arms that hugged him, pinioning his gun, were bear strong. Mackenzie put the butt of his free left hand under the fellow's nose, and pushed. The acolyte must let go. Mackenzie gave him a knee in the stomach, whirled, and ran.

45

There was not much further commotion behind him. Phil must have them under control. Mackenzie pelted along the hall, into the entry chamber. Where had that goddamn runner gone? He looked out the open entrance, onto the square. Sunlight hurt his eyes. His breath came in painful gulps, there was a stitch in his side, yeah, he was getting old.

Blue robes fluttered from a street. Mackenzie recognized the messenger. The youth pointed at this building. A gabble of his words drifted faintly through Mackenzie's pulse. There were seven or eight men with him—older men, nothing to mark their clothes . . . but Mackenzie knew a high-ranking officer when he saw one. The acolyte was dismissed. Those whom he had summoned crossed the square with long strides.

Terror knotted Mackenzie's bowels. He put it down. A Catamount didn't stampede, even from somebody who could turn him inside out with a look. He could do nothing about the wretchedness that followed, though. *If they clobber me, so much the better. I won't lie awake nights wondering how Laura is.*

The adepts were almost to the steps. Mackenzie trod forth. He swept his revolver in an arc. "Halt!" His voice sounded tiny in the stillness that brooded over the town.

They jarred to a stop and stood there in a group. He saw them enforce a catlike relaxation, and their faces became blank visors. None spoke. Finally Mackenzie was unable to keep silent.

"This place is hereby occupied under the laws of war," he said. "Go back to your quarters."

"What have you done with our leader?" asked a tall man. His voice was even but deeply resonant.

"Read my mind and find out," Mackenzie gibed. *No, you're being childish.* "He's okay, long's he keeps his nose clean. You too. Beat it."

"We do not wish to pervert psionics to violence," said the tall man. "Please do not force us."

"Your chief sent for you before we'd done anything," Mackenzie retorted. "Looks like violence was what he had in mind. On your way."

The Espers exchanged glances. The tall man nodded. His companions walked slowly off. "I would like to see Philosopher Gaines," the tall man said.

"You will pretty soon."

"Am I to understand that he is being held a prisoner?"

"Understand what you like." The other Espers were rounding the corner of the building. "I don't want to shoot. Go on back before I have to."

47

"An impasse of sorts," the tall man said. "Neither of us wishes to injure one whom he considers defenseless. Allow me to conduct you off these grounds."

Mackenzie wet his lips. Weather had chapped them rough. "If you can put a hex on me, go ahead," he challenged. "Otherwise scram."

"Well, I shall not hinder you from rejoining your men. It seems the easiest way of getting you to leave. But I most solemnly warn that any armed force which tries to enter will be annihilated."

Guess I had better go get the boys, at that. Phil can't mount guard on those guys forever.

The tall man went over to the hitching post. "Which of these horses is yours?" he asked blandly.

Almighty eager to get rid of me, isn't he— Holy hellfire! There must be a rear door!

Mackenzie spun on his heel. The Esper shouted. Mackenzie dashed back through the entry chamber. His boots threw echoes at him. No, not to the left, there's only the office that way. Right . . . around this corner—

A long hall stretched before him. A stairway curved from the middle. The other Espers were already on it.

"Halt!" Mackenzie called. "Stop or I'll shoot!"

The two men in the lead sped onward. The

rest turned and headed down again, toward him.

He fired with care, to disable rather than kill. The hall reverberated with the explosions. One after another they dropped, a bullet in leg or hip or shoulder. With such small targets, Mackenzie missed some shots. As the tall man, the last of them, closed in from behind, the hammer clicked on an empty chamber.

Mackenzie drew his saber and gave him the flat of it alongside the head. The Esper lurched. Mackenzie got past and bounded up the stair. It wound like something in a nightmare. He thought his heart was going to go to pieces.

At the end, an iron door opened on a landing. One man was fumbling with the lock. The other blue-robe attacked.

Mackenzie stuck his sword between the Esper's legs. As his opponent stumbled, the colonel threw a left hook to the jaw. The man sagged against the wall. Mackenzie grabbed the robe of the other and hurled him to the floor. "Get out," he rattled.

They pulled themselves together and glared at him. He thrust air with his blade. "From now on I aim to kill," he said.

"Get help, Dave," said the one who had been opening the door. "I'll watch him." The other went unevenly down the stairs. The first man stood out of saber reach. "Do you want to be destroyed?" he asked.

Mackenzie turned the knob at his back, but the door was still locked. "I don't think you can do it," he said. "Not without what's here."

The Esper struggled for self-control. They waited through minutes that stretched. Then a noise began below. The Esper pointed. "We have nothing but agricultural implements," he said, "but you have only that blade. Will you surrender?"

Mackenzie spat on the floor. The Esper went on down.

Presently the attackers came into view. There might be a hundred, judging from the hubbub behind them, but because of the curve Mackenzie could see no more than ten or fifteen—burly fieldhands, their robes tucked high and sharp tools aloft. The landing was too wide for defense. He advanced to the stairway, where they could only come at him two at a time.

A couple of sawtoothed hay knives led the assault. Mackenzie parried one blow and chopped. His edge went into meat and struck bone. Blood ran out, impossibly red, even in the dim light here. The man fell to all fours with a shriek. Mackenzie dodged a cut from the companion. Metal clashed on metal. The weapons locked. Mackenzie's arm was forced back. He looked into a broad suntanned face.

The side of his hand smote the young man's larynx. The Esper fell against the one behind and they went down together. It took a while to clear the tangle and resume action.

A pitchfork thrust for the colonel's belly. He managed to grab it with his left hand, divert the tines, and chop at the fingers on the shaft. A scythe gashed his right side. He saw his own blood but wasn't aware of pain. A flesh wound, no more. He swept his saber back and forth. The forefront retreated from its whistling menace. *But God, my knees are like rubber, I can't hold out another five minutes.*

A bugle sounded. There was a spatter of gunfire. The mob on the staircase congealed. Someone screamed.

Hoofs banged across the ground floor. A voice rasped: "Hold everything, there! Drop those weapons and come on down. First man tries anything gets shot."

Mackenzie leaned on his saber and fought for air. He hardly noticed the Espers melt away.

When he felt a little better, he went to one of the small windows and looked out. Horsemen were in the plaza. Not yet in sight, but nearing, he heard infantry.

Speyer arrived, followed by a sergeant of engineers and several privates. The major hurried to Mackenzie. "You okay, Jimbo? You been hurt!"

"A scratch," Mackenzie said. He was getting back his strength, though no sense of victory accompanied it, only the knowledge of aloneness. The injury began to sting. "Not worth a fuss. Look."

"Yes, I suppose you'll live. Okay, men, get that door open."

The engineers took forth their tools and assailed the lock with a vigor that must spring half from fear. "How'd you guys show up so soon?" Mackenzie asked.

"I thought there'd be trouble," Speyer said, "so when I heard shots I jumped through the window and ran around to my horse. That was just before those clodhoppers attacked you; I saw them gathering as I rode out. Our cavalry got in almost at once, of course, and the dogfaces weren't far behind."

"Any resistance?"

"No, not after we fired a few rounds in the air." Speyer glanced outside. "We're in full possession now."

Mackenzie regarded the door. "Well," he said, "I feel better about our having pulled guns on them in the office. Looks like their adepts really depend on plain old weapons, huh? And Esper communities aren't supposed to have arms. Their charters say to . . . That was a damn good guess of yours, Phil. How'd you do it?"

"I sort of wondered why the chief had to send a runner to fetch guys that claim to be telepaths. There we go!"

The lock jingled apart. The sergeant opened the door. Mackenzie and Speyer went into the great room under the dome.

They walked around for a long time, wordless, among shapes of metal and less identifiable substances. Nothing was familiar. Mackenzie paused at last before a helix which projected from a transparent cube. Formless darknesses swirled within the box, sparked as if with tiny stars.

"I figured maybe the Espers had found a cache of old-time stuff, from just before the Hellbombs," he said in a muffled voice. "Ultra-secret weapons that never got a chance to be used. But this doesn't look like it. Think so?"

"No," Speyer said. "It doesn't look to me as if these things were made by human beings at all."

"But do you not understand? They occupied a settlement! That proves to the world that Espers are not invulnerable. And to complete the catastrophe, they seized its arsenal."

"Have no fears about that. No untrained person can activate those instruments. The circuits are locked except in the presence of certain encephalic rhythms which result from conditioning. That same conditioning makes it impossible for the so-called adepts to reveal any of their knowledge to the uninitiated, no matter what may be done to them."

"Yes, I know that much. But it is not what I had in mind. What frightens me is the fact that the revelation will spread. Everyone will know the Esper adepts do not plumb unknown depths of the psyche after all, but merely have access to an advanced physical science. Not only will this lift rebel spirits, but worse, it will cause many, perhaps most of the Order's members to break away in disillusionment."

"Not at once. News travels slowly under present conditions. Also, Mwyr, you underestimate the ability of the human mind to ignore data which conflict with cherished beliefs."

"But—"

"Well, let us assume the worst. Let us suppose that faith is lost and the Order disintegrates. That will be a serious setback to the plan, but not a fatal one. Psionics was merely one bit of folklore we found potent enough to serve as the motivator of a new orientation toward life. There are others, for example the widespread belief in magic among the less educated classes. We can begin again on a different basis, if we must. The exact form of the creed is not important. It is only scaffolding for the real structure: a communal, anti-materialistic social group, to which more and more people will turn for sheer lack of anything else, as the coming empire breaks up. In the end, the new culture can and will discard whatever superstitions gave it the initial impetus."

"A hundred-year setback, at least."

"True. It would be much more difficult to introduce a radical alien element now, when the autochthonous society has developed strong institutions of its own, than it was in the past. I merely wish to reassure you that the task is not impossible. I do not actually propose to let matters go that far. The Espers can be salvaged."

"How?"

"We must intervene directly."

"Has that been computed as being unavoidable?"

"Yes. The matrix yields an unambiguous answer. I do not like it any better than you. But direct action occurs oftener than we tell neophytes in the schools. The most elegant procedure would of course be to establish such initial conditions in a society that its evolution along desired lines becomes automatic. Furthermore, that would let us close our minds to the distressing fact of our own blood guilt. Unfortunately, the Great Science does not extend down to the details of day-to-day practicality.

"In the present instance, we shall help to smash the reactionaries. The government will then proceed so harshly against its conquered opponents that many of those who accept the story about what was found at St. Helena will not live to spread the tale. The rest . . . well, they will be discredited by their own defeat. Admittedly, the story will linger for lifetimes, whispered here and there. But what of that? Those who believe in the Way will, as a rule, simply be strengthened in their faith, by the very process of denying such ugly rumors. As more and more persons, common citizens as well as Espers, reject materialism, the legend will seem more and more fantastic. It will seem obvious that certain ancients invented the tale to account for a fact that they in their ignorance were unable to comprehend."

"I see. . . ."

"You are not happy here, are you, Mwyr?"

"I cannot quite say. Everything is so distorted."

"Be glad you were not sent to one of the really alien planets."

"I might almost prefer that. There would be a hostile environment to think about. One could forget how far it is to home."

"Three years' travel."

"You say that so glibly. As if three shipboard years were not equal to fifty in cosmic time. As if we could expect a relief vessel daily, not once in a century. And . . . as if the region that our ships have explored *amounts to one chip out of this one galaxy!"*

"That region will grow until someday it engulfs the galaxy."

"Yes, yes, yes. I know. Why do you think I chose to become a psychodynamician? Why am I here, learning how to meddle with the destiny of a world where I do not belong? 'To create the union of sentient beings, each member species a step toward life's mastery of the universe.' Brave slogan! But in practice, it seems, only a chosen few races are to be allowed the freedom of that universe."

"Not so, Mwyr. Consider these ones with whom we are, as you say, meddling. Consider what use they made of nuclear energy when they had it. At the rate they are going, they will have it again within a century or two. Not long after that they will be building spaceships. Even granted that time lag attenuates the effects of interstellar contact, those effects are cumulative. So do you wish such a band of carnivores turned loose on the galaxy?

"No, let them become inwardly civilized first; then we shall see if they can be trusted. If not, they will at least be happy on their own planet, in a mode of life designed for them by the Great Science. Remember, they have an immemorial aspiration toward peace on earth; but that is

something they will never achieve by them-
selves. I do not pretend to be a very good
person, Mwyr. Yet this work that we are
doing makes me feel not altogether useless
in the cosmos."

Promotion was fast that year, casualties being so high. Captain Thomas Danielis was
raised to major for his conspicuous part in
putting down the revolt of the Los Angeles
citymen. Soon after occurred the Battle of
Maricopa, when the loyalists failed bloodily to
break the stranglehold of the Sierran rebels on
the San Joaquin Valley, and he was brevetted
lieutenant colonel. The army was ordered
northward and moved warily under the coast
ranges, half expecting attack from the east.
But the Brodskyites seemed too busy consoli-
dating their latest gains. The trouble came
from guerrillas and the hedgehog resistance of
bossman Stations. After one particularly stiff
clash, they stopped near Pinnacles for a
breather.

Danielis made his way through camp,
where tents stood in tight rows between the
guns and men lay about dozing, talking, gam-
bling, staring at the blank blue sky. The air
was hot, pungent with cookfire smoke, horses,
mules, dung, sweat, boot oil; the green of the
hills that lifted around the site was dulling
toward summer brown. He was idle until time
for the conference the general had called, but
restlessness drove him. *By now I'm a father*, he

thought, *and I've never seen my kid.*

At that, I'm lucky, he reminded himself. *I've got my life and limbs.* He remembered Jacobsen dying in his arms at Maricopa. You wouldn't have thought the human body could hold so much blood. Though maybe one was no longer human, when the pain was so great that one could do nothing but shriek until the darkness came.

And I used to think war was glamorous. Hunger, thirst, exhaustion, terror, mutilation, death, and forever the sameness, boredom grinding you down to an ox . . . I've had it. I'm going into business after the war. Economic integration, as the bossman system breaks up, yes, there'll be a lot of ways for a man to get ahead, but decently, without a weapon in his hand—Danielis realized he was repeating thoughts that were months old. What the hell else was there to think about, though?

The large tent where prisoners were interrogated lay near his path. A couple of privates were conducting a man inside. The fellow was blond, burly, and sullen. He wore a sergeant's stripes, but otherwise his only item of uniform was the badge of Warden Echevarry, bossman in this part of the coastal mountains. A lumberjack in peacetime, Danielis guessed from the look of him; a soldier in a private army whenever the interests of Echevarry were threatened; captured in yesterday's engagement.

On impulse, Danielis followed. He got into

the tent as Captain Lambert, chubby behind a portable desk, finished the preliminaries, and blinked in the sudden gloom.

"Oh." The intelligence officer started to rise. "Yes, sir?"

"At ease," Danielis said. "Just thought I'd listen in."

"Well, I'll try to put on a good show for you." Lambert reseated himself and looked at the prisoner, who stood with hunched shoulders and widespread legs between his guards. "Now, sergeant, we'd like to know a few things."

"I don't have to say nothing except name, rank, and home town," the man growled. "You got those."

"Um-m-m, that's questionable. You aren't a foreign soldier, you're in rebellion against the government of your own country."

"The hell I am! I'm an Echevarry man."

"So what?"

"So my Judge is whoever Echevarry says. He says Brodsky. That makes you the rebel."

"The law's been changed."

"Your mucking Fallon got no right to change any laws. Especially part of the Constitution. I'm no hillrunner, Captain. I went to school some. And every year our Warden reads his people the Constitution."

"Times have changed since it was drawn," Lambert said. His tone sharpened. "But I'm not going to argue with you. How many riflemen and how many archers in your company?"

Silence.

"We can make things a lot easier for you," Lambert said.

"I'm not asking you to do anything treasonable. All I want is to confirm some information I've already got."

The man shook his head angrily.

Lambert gestured. One of the privates stepped behind the captive, took his arm, and twisted a little.

"Echevarry wouldn't do that to me," he said through white lips.

"Of course not," Lambert said. "You're his man."

"Think I wanna be just a number on some list in Frisco? Damn right I'm my bossman's man!"

Lambert gestured again. The private twisted harder.

"Hold on, there," Danielis barked. "Stop that!"

The private let go, looking surprised. The prisoner drew a sobbing breath.

"I'm amazed at you, Captain Lambert," Danielis said. He felt his own face reddening. "If this has been your usual practice, there's going to be a court-martial."

"No sir," Lambert said in a small voice. "Honest. Only . . . they don't talk. Hardly any of them. What'm I supposed to do?"

"Follow the rules of war."

"With rebels?"

"Take that man away," Danielis ordered. The privates made haste to do so.

"Sorry, sir," Lambert muttered. "I guess . . . I guess I've lost too many buddies. I hate to lose more, simply for lack of information."

"Me too." A compassion rose in Danielis. He sat down on the table edge and began to roll a cigarette. "But you see, we aren't in a regular war. And so, by a curious paradox, we have to follow the conventions more carefully than ever before."

"I don't quite understand, sir."

Danielis finished the cigarette and gave it to Lambert: olive branch or something. He started another for himself. "The rebels aren't rebels by their own lights," he said. "They're being loyal to a tradition that we're trying to curb, eventually to destroy. Let's face it, the average bossman is a fairly good leader. He may be descended from some thug who grabbed power by strong-arm methods during the chaos, but by now his family's integrated itself with the region he rules. He knows it, and its people, inside out. He's there in the flesh, a symbol of the community and its achievements, its folkways and essential independence. If you're in trouble, you don't have to work through some impersonal bureaucracy, you go direct to your bossman. His duties are as clearly defined as your own, and a good deal more demanding, to balance his privi-

leges. He leads you in battle and in the cere-
monies that give color and meaning to life.
Your fathers and his have worked and played
together for two or three hundred years. The
land is alive with the memories of them. You
and he *belong*.

"Well, that has to be swept away, so we can
go on to a higher level. But we won't reach that
level by alienating everyone. We're not a con-
quering army; we're more like the Household-
er Guard putting down a riot in some city. The
opposition is part and parcel of our own society."

Lambert struck a match for him. He inhaled
and finished: "On a practical plane, I might
also remind you, Captain, that the federal
armed forces, Fallonite and Brodskyite together, are none too large. Little more than a
cadre, in fact. We're a bunch of younger sons,
countrymen who failed, poor citymen, adven-
turers, people who look to their regiment for
that sense of wholeness they've grown up to
expect and can't find in civilian life."

"You're too deep for me, sir, I'm afraid,"
Lambert said.

"Never mind," Danielis sighed. "Just bear
in mind, there are a good many more fighting
men outside the opposing armies than in. If
the bossmen could establish a unified command, that'd be the end of the Fallon government. Luckily, there's too much provincial
pride and too much geography between them

for this to happen—unless we outrage them beyond endurance. What we want the ordinary freeholder, and even the ordinary bossman, to think, is: 'Well, those Fallonites aren't such bad guys, and if I keep on the right side of them I don't stand to lose much, and should even be able to gain something at the expense of those who fight them to a finish.' You see?"

"Y-yes. I guess so."

"You're a smart fellow, Lambert. You don't have to beat information out of prisoners. Trick it out."

"I'll try, sir."

"Good." Danielis glanced at the watch that had been given him as per tradition, together with a sidearm, when he was first commissioned. (Such items were much too expensive for the common man. They had not been so in the age of mass production; and perhaps in the coming age—) "I have to go. See you around."

He left the tent feeling somewhat more cheerful than before. *No doubt I am a natural-born preacher*, he admitted, *and I never could quite join in the horseplay at mess, and a lot of jokes go completely by me; but if I can get even a few ideas across where they count, that's pleasure enough.* A strain of music came to him, some men and a banjo under a tree, and he found himself whistling along. It was good that this much morale remained, after Maricopa and a northward march whose purpose had not been divulged to anybody.

The conference tent was big enough to be called a pavilion. Two sentries stood at the entrance. Danielis was nearly the last to arrive, and found himself at the end of the table, opposite Brigadier General Perez. Smoke hazed the air and there was a muted buzz of conversation, but faces were taut.

When the blue-robed figure with a Yang and Yin on the breast entered, silence fell like a curtain. Danielis was astonished to recognize Philosopher Woodworth. He'd last seen the man in Los Angeles, and assumed he would stay at the Esper center there. Must have come here by special conveyance, under special orders. . . .

Perez introduced him. Both remained standing, under the eyes of the officers. "I have some important news for you, gentlemen," Perez said most quietly. "You may consider it an honor to be here. It means that in my judgment you can be trusted, first, to keep absolute silence about what you are going to hear, and second, to execute a vital operation of extreme difficulty." Danielis was made shockingly aware that several men were not present whose rank indicated they should be.

"I repeat," Perez said, "any breach of secrecy and the whole plan is ruined. In that case, the war will drag on for months or years. You know how bad our position is. You also know it will grow still worse as our stocks of those supplies the enemy now denies us are consumed. We could even be beaten. I'm not defeatist to say that, only realistic. We could lose the war.

"On the other hand, if this new scheme pans out, we may break the enemy's back this very month."

He paused to let that sink in before continuing:

"The plan was worked out by GHQ in conjunction with Esper Central in San Francisco some weeks ago. It's the reason we are headed north—" He let the gasp subside that ran through the stifling air. "Yes, you know that the Esper Order is neutral in political disputes. But you also know that it defends itself when attacked. And you probably know that an attack was made on it by the rebels. They seized the Napa Valley settlement and have been spreading malicious rumors about the Order since then. Would you like to comment on that, Philosopher Woodworth?"

The man in blue nodded and said coolly: "We've our own ways of findin' out things—intelligence service, you might say—so I can give y'all a report of the facts. St. Helena was assaulted at a time when most of its adepts were away, helpin' a new community get started out in Montana." *How did they travel so fast?* Danielis wondered. *Teleport, or what?*

"I don't know, myself, if the enemy knew about that or were just lucky. Anyhow, when the two or three adepts that were left came and warned them off, fightin' broke out and the adepts were killed before they could act." He smiled. "We don't claim to be immortal, except the way every livin' thing is immmortal. Nor infallible, either. So now St. Helena's occupied. We don't figure to take any immediate steps about that, because a lot of people in the community might get hurt.

"As for the yarns the enemy command's been handin' out, well, I reckon I'd do the same, if I had a chance like that. Everybody knows an adept can do things that nobody else can. Troops that realize they've done wrong to the Order are goin' to be scared of supernatural revenge. You're educated men here, and know there's nothin' supernatural involved, just a way to use the powers latent in most of us. You also know the Order doesn't believe in revenge. But the ordinary foot soldier doesn't think your way. His officers have got to restore his spirit somehow. So they fake some equipment and tell him that's what the adepts were really usin'—an advanced technology, sure, but only a set of machines that can be put out of action if you're brave, same as any other machine. That's what happened.

"Still, it is a threat to the Order; and we can't let an attack on our people go unpunished, either. So Esper Central has decided to help out your side. The sooner this war's over, the better for everybody."

A sigh gusted around the table, and a few exultant oaths. The hair stirred on Danielis' neck. Perez lifted a hand.

"Not too fast, please," the general said. "The adepts are not going to go around blasting your opponents for you. It was one hell of a tough decision for them to do as much as they agreed to. I, uh, understand that the, uh, personal development of every Esper will be set back many years by this much violence. They're making a big sacrifice.

"By their charter, they can use psionics to defend an establishment against attack. Okay . . . an assault on San Francisco will be construed as one on Central, their world headquarters."

The realization of what was to come was blinding to Danielis. He scarcely heard Perez' carefully dry continuation:

"Let's review the strategic picture. By now the enemy holds more than half of California, all of Oregon and Idaho, and a good deal of Washington. We, this army, we're using the last land access to San Francisco that we've got. The enemy hasn't tried to pinch that off yet, because the troops we pulled out of the north—those that aren't in the field at present —make a strong city garrison that'd sally out. He's collecting too much profit elsewhere to accept the cost.

"Nor can he invest the city with any hope of success. We still hold Puget Sound and the southern California ports. Our ships bring in ample food and munitions. His own sea power is much inferior to ours: chiefly schooners donated by coastal bossmen, operating out of Portland. He might overwhelm an occasional convoy, but he hasn't tried that so far because it isn't worth his trouble; there would be others, more heavily escorted. And of course he can't enter the Bay, with artillery and rocket emplacements on both sides of the Golden Gate. No, about all he can do is maintain some water communication with Hawaii and Alaska.

"Nevertheless, his ultimate object is San Francisco. It has to be—the seat of government and industry, the heart of the nation.

"Well, then, here's the plan. Our army is to engage the Sierra Command and its militia auxiliaries again, striking out of San Jose. That's a perfectly logical maneuver. Successful, it would cut his California forces in two. We know, in fact, that he is already concentrating men in anticipation of precisely such an attempt.

"We aren't going to succeed. We'll give him a good stiff battle and be thrown back. That's the hardest part: to feign a serious defeat, even convincing our own troops, and still maintain good order. We'll have a lot of details to thresh out about that.

"We'll retreat northward, up the Peninsula toward Frisco. The enemy is bound to pursue. It will look like a God-given chance to destroy us and get to the city walls.

"When he is well into the Peninsula, with the ocean on his left and the Bay on his right, we will outflank him and attack from the rear. The Esper adepts will be there to help. Suddenly he'll be caught, between us and the capital's land defenses. What the adepts don't wipe out, we will. Nothing will remain of the Sierra Command but a few garrisons. The rest of the war will be a mopping-up operation.

"It's a brilliant piece of strategy. Like all such, it's damn difficult to execute. Are you prepared to do the job?"

Danielis didn't raise his voice with the others. He was thinking too hard of Laura.

Northward and to the right there was some fighting. Cannon spoke occasionally, or a drumfire of rifles; smoke lay thin over the grass and the wind-gnarled live oaks which covered those hills. But down along the seacoast was only surf, blowing air, a hiss of sand across the dunes.

Mackenzie rode on the beach, where the footing was easiest and the view wildest. Most of his regiment were inland. But that was a wilderness: rough ground, woods, the snags of ancient homes, making travel slow and hard. Once this area had been densely populated, but the firestorm after the Hellbomb scrubbed it clean and today's reduced population could not make a go on such infertile soil. There didn't even seem to be any foremen near this left wing of the army.

The Rolling Stones had certainly not been given it for that reason. They could have borne the brunt at the center as well as those outfits which actually were there, driving the enemy back toward San Francisco. They had been blooded often enough in this war, when they operated out of Calistoga to help expel the Fallonites from northern California. So thoroughly had that job been done that now only a skeleton force need remain in charge. Nearly the whole Sierra Command had gathered at Modesto, met the northward-moving opposition army that struck at them out of San Jose, and sent it in a shooting retreat. Another day or so, and the white city should appear before their eyes.

And there the enemy will be sure to make a stand, Mackenzie thought, *with the garrison to reinforce him. And his positions will have to be shelled; maybe we'll have to take the place street by street. Laura, kid, will you be alive at the end?*

Of course, maybe it won't happen that way. Maybe my scheme'll work and we'll win easy— What a horrible word "maybe" is! He slapped his hands together with a pistol sound.

Speyer threw him a glance. The major's

people were safe; he'd even been able to visit them at Mount Lassen, after the northern campaign was over. "Rough," he said.

"Rough on everybody," Mackenzie said with a thick anger. "This is a filthy war."

Speyer shrugged. "No different from most, except that this time Pacificans are on the receiving as well as the giving end."

"You know damn well I never liked the business, anyplace."

"What man in his right mind does?"

"When I want a sermon I'll ask for one."

"Sorry," said Speyer, and meant it.

"I'm sorry too," said Mackenzie, instantly contrite. "Nerves on edge. Damnation! I could almost wish for some action."

"Wouldn't be surprised if we got some. This whole affair smells wrong to me."

Mackenzie looked around him. On the right the horizon was bounded by hills, beyond which the low but massive San Bruno range lifted. Here and there he spied one of his own squads, afoot or ahorse. Overhead sputtered a plane. But there was plenty of concealment for a redoubt. Hell could erupt at any minute . . . though necessarily a small hell, quickly reduced by howitzer or bayonet, casualties light. (Huh! Every one of those light casualties was a man dead, with women and children to weep for him, or a man staring at the fragment of his arm, or a man with eyes and face gone in a burst of shot, and what kind of unsoldierly thoughts were these?)

Seeking comfort, Mackenzie glanced left. The ocean rolled greenish-gray, glittering far out, rising and breaking in a roar of white combers closer to land. He smelled salt and kelp. A few gulls mewed above dazzling sands. There was no sail or smoke-puff—only emptiness. The convoys from Puget Sound to San Francisco and the lean swift ships of the coastal bossmen were miles beyond the curve of the world.

Which was as it should be. Maybe things were working out okay on the high waters. One could only try, and hope. And . . . it had been his suggestion, James Mackenzie speaking at the conference General Cruikshank held between the battles of Mariposa and San Jose; the same James Mackenzie who had first proposed that the Sierra Command come down out of the mountains, and who had exposed the gigantic fraud of Esperdom, and succeeded in playing down for his men the fact that behind the fraud lay a mystery one hardly dared think about. He would endure in the chronicles, that colonel, they would sing ballads about him for half a thousand years.

Only it didn't feel that way. James Mackenzie knew he was not much more than average bright under the best of conditions, now dull-minded with weariness and terrified of his daughter's fate. For himself he was haunted by the fear of certain crippling wounds. Often he had to drink himself to sleep. He was shaved, because an officer must maintain appearances, but realized very well that if he hadn't had an orderly to do the job for him he would be as shaggy as any buck private. His uniform was faded and threadbare, his body stank and itched, his mouth yearned for tobacco but there had been some trouble in the commissariat and they were lucky to eat. His achievements amounted to patchwork jobs carried out in utter confusion, or to slogging like this and wishing only for an end to the whole mess. One day, win or lose, his body would give out on him—he could feel the machinery wearing to pieces, arthritic twinges, shortness of breath, dozing off in the middle of things— and the termination of himself would be as undignified and lonely as that of every other human slob. Hero? What an all-time laugh!

He yanked his mind back to the immediate situation. Behind him a core of the regiment accompanied the artillery along the beach, a thousand men with motorized gun carriages, caissons, mule-drawn wagons, a few trucks, one precious armored car. They were a dun mass topped with helmets, in loose formation, rifles or bows to hand. The sand deadened their footfalls, so that only the surf and the wind could be heard. But whenever the wind sank, Mackenzie caught the tune of the hex corps: a dozen leathery older men, mostly Indians, carrying the wands of power and whistling together the Song Against Witches. He took no stock in magic himself, yet when that sound came to him the skin crawled along his backbone.

Everything's in good order, he insisted. *We're doing fine.*

Then: *But Phil's right. This is a screwball business. The enemy should have fought through to a southward line of retreat, not let themselves be boxed.*

Captain Hulse galloped close. Sand spurted when he checked his horse. "Patrol report, sir."

"Well?" Mackenzie realized he had almost shouted. "Go ahead."

"Considerable activity observed about five miles northeast. Looks like a troop headed our way."

Mackenzie stiffened. "Haven't you anything more definite than that?"

"Not so far, with the ground so broken."

"Get some aerial reconnaissance there, for Pete's sake!"

"Yes, sir. I'll throw out more scouts, too."

"Carry on here, Phil." Mackenzie headed toward the radio truck. He carried a minicom in his saddlebag, of course, but San Francisco had been continuously jamming on all bands and you needed a powerful set to punch a signal even a few miles. Patrols must communicate by messenger.

He noticed that the firing inland had slaked off. There were decent roads in the interior Peninsula a ways further north, where some resettlement had taken place. The enemy, still in possession of that area, could use them to effect rapid movements.

If they withdrew their center and hit our flanks, where we're weakest—

A voice from field HQ, barely audible through the squeals and buzzes, took his report and gave back what had been seen elsewhere. Large maneuvers right and left, yes, it did seem as if the Fallonites were going to try a breakthrough. Could be a feint, though. The main body of the Sierrans must remain where it was until the situation became clearer. The Rolling Stones must hold out a while on their own.

"Will do." Mackenzie returned to the head of his columns. Speyer nodded grimly at the word.

"Better get prepared, hadn't we?"

"Uh-huh." Mackenzie lost himself in a welter of commands, as officer after officer rode to him. The outlying sections were to be pulled in. The beach was to be defended, with the high ground immediately above.

Men scurried, horses neighed, guns trundled about. The scout plane returned, flying low enough to get a transmission through: yes, definitely an attack on the way; hard to tell how big a force, through the damned tree cover and down in the damned arroyos, but it might well be at brigade strength.

Mackenzie established himself on a hilltop with his staff and runners. A line of artillery stretched beneath him, across the strand. Cavalry waited behind them, lances agleam, an infantry company for support. Otherwise the foot soldiers had faded into the landscape. The sea boomed its own cannonade, and gulls began to gather as if they knew there would be meat before long.

"Think we can hold them?" Speyer asked.

"Sure," Mackenzie said. "If they come down the beach, we'll enfilade them, as well as shooting up their front. If they come higher, well, that's a textbook example of defensible terrain. 'Course, if another troop punches through the lines further inland, we'll be cut off, but that isn't our worry right now."

"They must hope to get around our army and attack our rear."

"Guess so. Not too smart of them, though. We can approach Frisco just as easily fighting backwards as forwards."

"Unless the city garrison makes a sally."

"Even then. Total numerical strengths are about equal, and we've got more ammo and alky. Also a lot of bossman militia for auxiliaries, who're used to disorganized warfare in hilly ground."

"If we do whip them—" Speyer shut his lips together.

"Go on," Mackenzie said.

"Nothing."

"The hell it is. You were about to remind me of the next step: how do we take the city without too high a cost to both sides? Well, I happen to know we've got a hole card to play there, which might help."

Speyer turned pitying eyes away from Mackenzie. Silence fell on the hilltop.

It was an unconscionably long time before the enemy came in view, first a few outriders far down the dunes, then the body of him, pouring from the ridges and gullies and woods. Reports flickered about Mackenzie—a powerful force, nearly twice as big as ours, but with little artillery; by now badly short of fuel, they must depend far more than we on animals to move their equipment. They were evidently going to charge, accept losses in order to get sabers and bayonets among the Rolling Stones' cannon. Mackenzie issued his directions accordingly.

The hostiles formed up, a mile or so distant. Through his field glasses Mackenzie recognized them, red sashes of the Madera Horse, green and gold pennon of the Dagos, fluttering in the iodine wind. He'd campaigned with

both outfits in the past. It was treacherous to
remember that Ives favored a blunt wedge
formation and use the fact against him . . .
One enemy armored car and some fieldpieces,
light horsedrawn ones, gleamed wickedly in
the sunlight.

Bugles blew shrill. The Fallonite cavalry
laid lance in rest and started trotting. They
gathered speed as they went, a canter, a
gallop, until the earth trembled with them.
Then their infantry got going, flanked by its
guns. The car rolled along between the first
and second line of foot. Oddly, it had no
rocket launcher on top or repeater barrels
thrust from the fire slits. Those were good
troops, Mackenzie thought, advancing in close
order with that ripple down the ranks which
bespoke veterans. He hated what must happen.

His defense waited immobile on the sand.
Fire crackled from the hillsides, where mortar
squads and riflemen crouched. A rider top-
pled, a dogface clutched his belly and went to
his knees, their companions behind moved
forward to close the lines again. Mackenzie
looked to his howitzers. Men stood tensed at
sights and lanyards. Let the foe get well in
range—There! Yamaguchi, mounted just rearward of the gunners, drew his saber and
flashed the blade downward. Cannon bellowed. Fire spurted through smoke, sand
gouted up, shrapnel sleeted over the charging

force. At once the gun crews fell into the rhythm of reloading, relaying, refiring, the steady three rounds per minute which conserved barrels and broke armies. Horses screamed in their own tangled red guts. But not many had been hit. The Madera cavalry continued in full gallop. Their lead was so close now that Mackenzie's glasses picked out a face, red, freckled, a ranch boy turned trooper, his mouth stretched out of shape as he yelled.

The archers behind the defending cannon let go. Arrows whistled skyward, flight after flight, curved past the gulls and down again. Flame and smoke ran ragged in the wiry hill grass, out of the ragged-leaved live oak copses. Men pitched to the sand, many still hideously astir, like insects that had been stepped on. The fieldpieces on the enemy left flank halted, swiveled about, and spat return fire. Futile . . . but God, their officer had courage! Mackenzie saw the advancing lines waver. An attack by his own horse and foot, down the beach, ought to crumple them. "Get ready to move," he said into his minicom. He saw his men poise. The cannon belched anew.

The oncoming armored car slowed to a halt. Something within it chattered, loud enough to hear through the explosions.

A blue-white sheet ran over the nearest hill. Mackenzie shut half-blinded eyes. When he opened them again, he saw a grass fire through the crazy patterns of after-image. A Rolling Stone burst from cover, howling, his clothes ablaze. The man hit the sand and rolled over. That part of the beach lifted in one monster wave, crested twenty feet high, and smashed across the hill. The burning soldier vanished in the avalanche that buried his comrades.

"*Psi blast!*" someone screamed, thin and horrible, through chaos and ground-shudder. "The Espers—"

Unbelievably, a bugle sounded and the Sierran cavalry lunged forward. Past their own guns, on against the scattering opposition . . . and horses and riders rose into the air, tumbled in a giant's invisible whirligig, crashed bone-breakingly to earth again. The second rank of lancers broke. Mounts reared, pawed the air, wheeled and fled in every direction.

A terrible deep hum filled the sky. Mackenzie saw the world as if through a haze, as if his brain were being dashed back and forth between the walls of his skull. Another glare ran across the hills, higher this time, burning men alive.

"They'll wipe us out," Speyer called, a dim voice that rose and fell on the air tides. "They'll re-form as we stampede—"

"No!" Mackenzie shouted. "The adepts must be in that car. Come on!"

Most of his horse had recoiled on their own artillery, one squealing, trampling wreck. The infantry stood rigid, but about to bolt. A glance thrown to his right showed Mackenzie how the enemy themselves were in confusion, this had been a terrifying surprise to them too, but as soon as they got over the shock they'd advance and there'd be nothing left to stop them . . . It was as if another man spurred his mount. The animal fought, foam-flecked with panic. He slugged its head around, brutally, and dug in spurs. They rushed down the hill toward the guns.

He needed all his strength to halt the gelding before the cannon mouths. A man slumped dead by this piece, though there was no mark on him. Mackenzie jumped to the ground. His steed bolted.

He hadn't time to worry about that. Where was help? "Come here!" His yell was lost in the riot. But suddenly another man was beside him, Speyer, snatching up a shell and slamming it into the breach. Mackenzie squinted through the telescope, took a bearing by guess and feel. He could see the Esper car where it squatted among dead and hurt. At this distance it looked too small to have blackened acres.

Speyer helped him lay the howitzer. He jerked the lanyard. The gun roared and sprang. The shell burst a few yards short of target, sand spurted and metal fragments whined.

Speyer had the next one loaded. Mackenzie

aimed and fired. Overshot this time, but not by much. The car rocked. Concussion might have hurt the Espers inside; at least, the psi blasts had stopped. But it was necessary to strike before the foe got organized again.

He ran toward his own regimental car. The door gaped, the crew had fled. He threw himself into the driver's seat. Speyer clanged the door shut and stuck his face in the hood of the rocket-launcher periscope. Mackenzie raced the machine forward. The banner on its rooftop snapped in the wind.

Speyer aimed the launcher and pressed the firing button. The missile burned across intervening yards and exploded. The other car lurched on its wheels. A hole opened in its side.

If the boys will only rally and advance— Well, if they don't, I'm done for anyway. Mackenzie squealed to a stop, flung open the door and leaped out. Curled, blackened metal framed his entry. He wriggled through, into murk and stenches.

Two Espers lay there. The driver was dead, a chunk of steel through his breast. The other one, the adept, whimpered among his unhuman instruments. His face was hidden by blood. Mackenzie pitched the corpse on its side and pulled off the robe. He snatched a curving tube of metal and tumbled back out.

Speyer was still in the undamaged car, firing

repeaters at those hostiles who ventured near. Mackenzie jumped onto the ladder of the disabled machine, climbed to its roof and stood erect. He waved the blue robe in one hand and the weapon he did not understand in the other. "Come on, you sons!" he shouted, tiny against the sea wind. "We've knocked 'em out for you! Want your breakfast in bed too?"

One bullet buzzed past his ear. Nothing else. Most of the enemy, horse and foot, stayed frozen. In that immense stillness he could not tell if he heard surf or the blood in his own veins.

Then a bugle called. The hex corps whistled triumphantly; their tomtoms thuttered. A ragged line of his infantry began to move toward him. More followed. The cavalry joined them, man by man and unit by unit, on their flanks. Soldiers ran down the smoking hillsides.

Mackenzie sprang to sand again and into his car. "Let's get back," he told Speyer. "We got a battle to finish."

"Shut up!" Tom Danielis said.

Philosopher Woodworth stared at him. Fog swirled and dripped in the forest, hiding the land and the brigade, gray nothingness through which came a muffled noise of men and horses and wheels, an isolated and infinitely weary sound. The air was cold, and clothing hung heavy on the skin.

"Sir," protested Major Lescarbault. The

eyes were wide and shocked in his gaunted face.

"I dare tell a ranking Esper to stop quacking about a subject of which he's totally ignorant?" Danielis answered. "Well, it's past time that somebody did."

Woodworth recovered his poise. "All I said, son, was that we should consolidate our adepts and strike the Brodskyite center," he reproved. "What's wrong with that?"

Danielis clenched his fists. "Nothing," he said, "except it invites a worse disaster than you've brought on us yet."

"A setback or two," Lescarbault argued. "They did rout us on the west, but we turned their flank here by the Bay."

"With the net result that their main body pivoted, attacked, and split us in half," Danielis snapped. "The Espers have been scant use since then . . . now the rebels know they need vehicles to transport their weapons, and can be killed. Artillery zeroes in on their positions, or bands of woodsmen hit and run, leaving them dead, or the enemy simply goes around any spot where they're known to be. We haven't got enough adepts!"

"That's why I proposed gettin' them in one group, too big to withstand," Woodworth said.

"And too cumbersome to be of any value," Danielis replied. He felt more than a little sickened, knowing how the Order had cheated him his whole life; yes, he thought, that was

85

the real bitterness, not the fact that the adepts had failed to defeat the rebels—by failing, essentially, to break their spirit—but the fact that the adepts were only someone else's cat's paws and every gentle, earnest soul in every Esper community was only someone's dupe.

Wildly he wanted to return to Laura— there'd been no chance thus far to see her— Laura and the kid, the last honest reality this fog-world had left him. He mastered himself and went on more evenly.

"The adepts, what few of them survive, will of course be helpful in defending San Francisco. An army free to move around in the field can deal with them, one way or another, but your . . . your weapons can repel an assault on the city walls. So that's where I'm going to take them."

Probably the best he could do. There was no word from the northern half of the loyalist army. Doubtless they'd withdrawn to the capital, suffering heavy losses en route. Radio jamming continued, hampering friendly and hostile communications alike. He had to take action, either retreat southward or fight his way through to the city. The latter course seemed wisest. He didn't believe that Laura had much to do with his choice.

"I'm no adept myself," Woodworth said. "I can't call them mind to mind."

"You mean you can't use their equivalent of radio," Danielis said brutally. "Well, you've got an adept in attendance. Have him pass the word."

Woodworth flinched. "I hope," he said, "I hope you understand this came as a surprise to me too."

"Oh, yes, certainly, Philosopher," Lescarbault said unbidden.

Woodworth swallowed. "I still hold with the Way and the Order," he said harshly. "There's nothin' else I can do. Is there? The Grand Seeker has promised a full explanation when this is over." He shook his head. "Okay, son, I'll do what I can."

A certain compassion touched Danielis as the blue robe disappeared into the fog. He rapped his orders the more severely.

Slowly his command got going. He was with the Second Brigade; the rest were strewn over the Peninsula in the fragments into which the rebels had knocked them. He hoped the equally scattered adepts, joining him on his march through the San Bruno range, would guide some of those units to him. But most, wandering demoralized, were sure to surrender to the first rebels they came upon.

He rode near the front, on a muddy road that snaked over the highlands. His helmet was a monstrous weight. The horse stumbled beneath him, exhausted by—how many days? —of march, countermarch, battle, skirmish, thin rations or none, heat and cold and fear, in an empty land. Poor beast, he'd see that it got proper treatment when they reached the city. That all those poor beasts behind him did, after trudging and fighting and trudging again until their eyes were filmed with fatigue.

There'll be chance enough for rest in San Francisco. We're impregnable there, walls and cannon and the Esper machines to landward, the sea that feeds us at our backs. We can recover our strength, regroup our forces, bring fresh troops down from Washington and up from the south by water. The war isn't decided yet . . . God help us.

I wonder if it will ever be.

And then, will Jimbo Mackenzie come to see us, sit by the fire and swap yarns about what we did? Or talk about something else, anything else? If not, that's too high a price for victory.

Maybe not too high a price for what we've learned, though. Strangers on this planet . . . what else could have forged those weapons? The adepts will talk if I myself have to torture them till they do. But Danielis remembered tales muttered in the fisher huts of his boyhood, after dark, when ghosts walked in old men's minds. Before the holocaust there had been legends about the stars, and the legends lived on. He didn't know if he would be able to look again at the night sky without a shiver.

This damned fog—

Hoofs thudded. Danielis half drew his side-arm. But the rider was a scout of his own, who raised a drenched sleeve in salute. "Colonel, an enemy force about ten miles ahead by road. Big."

So we'll have to fight now. "Do they seem aware of us?"

"No, sir. They're proceeding east along the ridge there."

"Probably figure to occupy the Candlestick Park ruins," Danielis murmured. His body was too tired for excitement. "Good stronghold, that. Very well, Corporal." He turned to Lescarbault and issued instructions.

The brigade formed itself in the formlessness. Patrols went out. Information began to flow back, and Danielis sketched a plan that ought to work. He didn't want to try for a decisive engagement, only brush the enemy aside and discourage them from pursuit. His men must be spared, as many as possible, for the city defense and the eventual counteroffensive.

Lescarbault came back. "Sir! The radio jamming's ended!"

"What?" Danielis blinked, not quite comprehending.

"Yes, sir. I've been using a minicom—" Lescarbault lifted the wrist on which his tiny transceiver was strapped—"for very short-range work, passing the battalion commanders their orders. The interference stopped a couple of minutes ago. Clear as daylight."

Danielis pulled the wrist toward his own mouth. "Hello, hello, radio wagon, this is the C.O. You read me?"

"Yes, sir," said the voice.

"They turned off the jammer in the city for a reason. Get me the open military band."

"Yes, sir." Pause, while men mumbled and water runneled unseen in the arroyos. A wraith smoked past Danielis' eyes. Drops coursed off his helmet and down his collar. The horse's mane hung sodden.

Like the scream of an insect:

"—here at once! Every unit in the field, get to San Francisco at once! We're under attack by sea!"

Danielis let go Lescarbault's arm. He stared into emptiness while the voice wailed on and forever on.

"—bombarding Potrero Point. Decks jammed with troops. They must figure to make a landing there—"

Danielis' mind raced ahead of the words. It was as if Esp were no lie, as if he scanned the beloved city himself and felt her wounds in his own flesh. There was no fog around the Gate, of course, or so detailed a description could not have been given. Well, probably some streamers of it rolled in under the rusted remnants of the bridge, themselves like snow-banks against blue-green water and brilliant sky. But most of the Bay stood open to the sun.

On the opposite shore lifted the Eastbay hills, green with gardens and agleam with villas; and Marin shouldered heavenward across the strait, looking to the roofs and walls and heights that were San Francisco. The convoy had gone between the coast defenses that could have smashed it, an unusually large convoy and not on time: but still the familiar big-bellied hulls, white sails, occasional fuming stacks, that kept the city fed. There had been an explanation about trouble with commerce raiders; and the fleet was passed on into the Bay, where San Francisco had no walls. Then the gun covers were taken off and the holds vomited armed men.

Yes, they did seize a convoy, those piratical schooners. Used radio jamming of their own; together with ours, that choked off any cry of warning. They threw our supplies overboard and embarked the bossman militia. Some spy or traitor gave them the recognition signals. Now the capital lies open to them, her garrison stripped, hardly an adept left in Esper Central, the Sierrans thrusting against her southern gates, and Laura without me.

"We're coming!" Danielis yelled. His brigade groaned into speed behind him. They struck with a desperate ferocity that carried them deep into enemy positions and then stranded them in separated groups. It became knife and saber in the fog. But Danielis, because he led the charge, had already taken a grenade on his breast.

East and south, in the harbor district and at the wreck of the Peninsula wall, there was still some fighting. As he rode higher, Mackenzie saw how those parts were dimmed by smoke, which the wind scattered to show rubble that had been houses. The sound of firing drifted to him. But otherwise the city shone untouched, roofs and white walls in a web of streets, church spires raking the sky like masts, Federal House on Nob Hill and the Watchtower on Telegraph Hill as he remembered them from childhood visits. The Bay glittered insolently beautiful.

But he had no time for admiring the view, nor for wondering where Laura huddled. The attack on Twin Peaks must be swift, for surely Esper Central would defend itself.

On the avenue climbing the opposite side of those great humps, Speyer led half the Rolling Stones. (Yamaguchi lay dead on a pockmarked beach.) Mackenzie himself was taking this side. Horses clopped along Portola, between blankly shuttered mansions; guns trundled and creaked, boots knocked on pavement, moccasins slithered, weapons rattled, men breathed heavily and the hex corps whistled against unknown demons. But silence overwhelmed the noise, echoes trapped it and let it die. Mackenzie recollected nightmares when he fled down a corridor which had no end. *Even if they don't cut loose at us, he thought bleakly, we've got to seize their place before our nerve gives out.*

Twin Peaks Boulevard turned off Portola and wound steeply to the right. The houses ended; wild grasses alone covered the quasi-sacred hills, up to the tops where stood the buildings forbidden to all but adepts. Those two soaring, iridescent, fountainlike skyscrapers had been raised by night, within a matter of weeks. Something like a moan stirred at Mackenzie's back.

"Bugler, sound the advance. On the double!"

A child's jeering, the notes lifted and were lost. Sweat stung Mackenzie's eyes. If he failed and was killed, that didn't matter too much . . . after everything which had happened . . . but the regiment, the regiment—

Flame shot across the street, the color of hell. There went a hiss and a roar. The pavement lay trenched, molten, smoking and reeking. Mackenzie wrestled his horse to a standstill. *A warning only. But if they had enough adepts to handle us, would they bother trying to scare us off?* "Artillery, open fire!"

The field guns bellowed together, not only howitzers but motorized 75s taken along from Alemany Gate's emplacements. Shells went overhead with a locomotive sound. They burst on the walls above and the racket thundered back down the wind.

Mackenzie tensed himself for an Esper blast, but none came. Had they knocked out the final defensive post in their own first barrage? Smoke cleared from the heights and he saw that the colors which played in the tower were dead and that wounds gaped across loveliness, showing unbelievably thin framework. It was like seeing the bones of a woman murdered by his hand.

Quick, though! He issued a string of commands and led the horse and foot on. The battery stayed where it was, firing and firing with hysterical fury. The dry brown grass started to burn, as red-hot fragments scattered across the slope. Through mushroom bursts, Mackenzie saw the building crumble. Whole sheets of facing broke and fell to earth. The skeleton vibrated, took a direct hit and sang in metal agony, slumped and twisted apart.

What was that which stood within?

There were no separate rooms, no floors, nothing but girders, enigmatic machines, here and there a globe still aglow like a minor sun. The structure had enclosed something nearly as tall as itself, a finned and shining column, almost like a rocket shell but impossibly huge and fair.

Their spaceship, Mackenzie thought in the clamor. *Yes, of course, the ancients had begun making spaceships, and we always figured we would again someday. This, though—!*

The archers lifted a tribal screech. The riflemen and cavalry took it up, crazy, jubilant, the howl of a beast of prey. *By Satan, we've whipped the stars themselves!* As they burst onto the hillcrest, the shelling stopped, and their yells overrode the wind. Smoke was acrid as blood smell in their nostrils.

A few dead blue-robers could be seen in the debris. Some half-dozen survivors milled toward the ship. A bowman let fly. His arrow glanced off the landing gear but brought the Espers to a halt. Troopers poured over the shards to capture them.

Mackenzie reined in. Something that was not human lay crushed near a machine. Its blood was deep violet color. *When the people have seen this, that's the end of the Order.* He felt no triumph. At St. Helena he had come to appreciate how fundamentally good the believers were.

But this was no moment for regret, or for wondering how harsh the future would be with man taken entirely off the leash. The building on the other peak was still intact. He had to consolidate his position here, then help Phil if need be.

However, the minicom said, "Come on and join me, Jimbo. The fracas is over," before he had completed his task. As he rode along toward Speyer's place, he saw a Pacific States flag flutter up the mast on that skyscraper's top.

Guards stood awed and nervous at the portal. Mackenzie dismounted and walked inside. The entry chamber was a soaring, shimmering fantasy of colors and arches, through which men moved troll-like. A corporal led him down a hall. Evidently this building had been used for quarters, offices, storage, and less understandable purposes. . . . There was a room whose door had been blown down with dynamite. The fluid abstract murals were stilled, scarred, and sooted. Four ragged troopers pointed guns at the two beings whom Speyer was questioning.

One slumped at something that might answer to a desk. The avian face was buried in seven-fingered hands and the rudimentary wings quivered with sobs. *Are they able to cry, then?* Mackenzie thought, astonished, and had a sudden wish to take the being in his arms and offer what comfort he was able.

The other one stood erect in a robe of woven metal. Great topaz eyes met Speyer's from a seven-foot height, and the voice turned accented English into music.

"—a G-type star some fifty light-years hence. It is barely visible to the naked eye, though not in this hemisphere."

The major's fleshless, bristly countenance jutted forward as if to peck. "When do you expect reinforcements?"

"There will be no other ship for almost a century, and it will only bring personnel. We are isolated by space and time; few can come to work here, to seek to build a bridge of minds across that gulf—"

"Yeah," Speyer nodded prosaically. "The lightspeed limit. I thought so. If you're telling the truth."

The being shuddered. "Nothing is left for us but to speak truth, and pray that you will understand and help. Revenge, conquest, any form of mass violence is impossible when so much space and time lies between. Our labor has been done in the mind and heart. It is not too late, even now. The most crucial facts can still be kept hidden—oh, listen to me, for the sake of your unborn!"

Speyer nodded to Mackenzie. "Everything okay?" he said. "We got us a full bag here. About twenty left alive, this fellow the bossman. Seems like they're the only ones on Earth."

"We guessed there couldn't be many," the colonel said. His tone and his feelings were alike ashen. "When we talked it over, you and me, and tried to figure what our clues meant. They'd have to be few, or they'd've operated more openly."

"Listen, listen," the being pleaded. "We came in love. Our dream was to lead you—to make you lead yourselves—toward peace, fulfillment . . . Oh, yes, we would also gain,

gain yet another race with whom we could someday converse as brothers. But there are many races in the universe. It was chiefly for your own tortured sakes that we wished to guide your future."

"That controlled history notion isn't original with you," Speyer grunted. "We've invented it for ourselves now and then on Earth. The last time it led to the Hellbombs. No, thanks!"

"But we *know!* The Great Science predicts with absolute certainty—"

"Predicted this?" Speyer waved a hand at the blackened room.

"There are fluctuations. We are too few to control so many savages in every detail. But do you not wish an end to war, to all your ancient sufferings? I offer you that for your help today."

"You succeeded in starting a pretty nasty war yourselves," Speyer said.

The being twisted its fingers together. "That was an error. The plan remains, the only way to lead your people toward peace. I, who have traveled between suns, will get down before your boots and beg you—"

"Stay put!" Speyer flung back. "If you'd come openly, like honest folk, you'd have found some to listen to you. Maybe enough, even. But no, your do-gooding had to be subtle and crafty. You knew what was right for us. We weren't entitled to say anything in the matter. God in heaven, I've never heard anything so arrogant!"

The being lifted its head. "Do you tell children the whole truth?"

"As much as they're ready for."

"Your child-culture is not ready to hear these truths."

"Who qualified you to call us children—besides yourselves?"

"How do you know you are an adult?"

"By trying adult jobs and finding out if I can handle them. Sure, we make some ghastly blunders, we humans. But they're our own. And we learn from them. You're the ones who won't learn, you and that damned psychological science you were bragging about, that wants to fit every living mind into the one frame it can understand.

"You wanted to re-establish the centralized state, didn't you? Did you ever stop to think that maybe feudalism is what suits man? Some one place to call our own, and belong to, and be part of; a community with traditions and honor; a chance for the individual to make decisions that count; a bulwark for liberty against the central overlords, who'll always want more and more power; a thousand different ways to live. We've always built supercountries, here on Earth, and we've always knocked them apart again. I think maybe the whole idea is wrong. And maybe this time we'll try something better. Why not a world of little states, too well rooted to dissolve in a nation, too small to do much harm—slowly rising above petty jealousies and spite, but keeping their identities—a thousand separate approaches to our problems. Maybe then we can solve a few of them . . . for ourselves!"

"You will never do so," the being said. "You will be torn in pieces all over again."

"That's what you think. I think otherwise. But whichever is right—and I bet this is too big a universe for either of us to predict—we'll have made a free choice on Earth. I'd rather be dead than domesticated.

"The people are going to learn about you as soon as Judge Brodsky's been reinstated. No, sooner. The regiment will hear today, the city tomorrow, just to make sure no one gets ideas about suppressing the truth again. By the time your next spaceship comes, we'll be ready for it: in our own way, whatever that is."

The being drew a fold of robe about its head. Speyer turned to Mackenzie. His face was wet. "Anything . . . you want to say . . . Jimbo?"

"No," Mackenzie mumbled. "Can't think of anything. Let's get our command organized here. I don't expect we'll have to fight any more, though. It seems to be about ended down there."

"Sure." Speyer drew an uneven breath. "The enemy troops elsewhere are bound to capitulate. They've got nothing left to fight for. We can start patching up pretty soon."

There was a house with a patio whose wall was covered by roses. The street outside had not yet come back to life, so that silence dwelt here under the yellow sunset. A maidservant showed Mackenzie through the back door and departed. He walked toward Laura, who sat on a bench beneath a willow. She watched him approach but did not rise. One hand rested on a cradle.

He stopped and knew not what to say. How thin she was!

Presently she told him, so low he could scarcely hear: "Tom's dead."

"Oh, no." Darkness came and went before his eyes.

"I learned the day before yesterday, when a few of his men straggled home. He was killed in the San Bruno."

Mackenzie did not dare join her, but his legs would not upbear him. He sat down on the flagstones and saw curious patterns in their arrangement. There was nothing else to look at.

Her voice ran on above him, toneless: "Was it worth it? Not only Tom, but so many others, killed for a point of politics?"

"More than that was at stake," he said.

"Yes, I heard on the radio. I still can't understand how it was worth it. I've tried very hard, but I can't."

He had no strength left to defend himself. "Maybe you're right, duck. I wouldn't know."

"I'm not sorry for myself," she said. "I still have Jimmy. But Tom was cheated out of so much."

He realized all at once that there was a baby, and he ought to take his grandchild to him and think thoughts about life going on into the future. But he was too empty.

"Tom wanted him named after you," she said.

Did you, Laura? he wondered. Aloud: "What are you going to do now?"

"I'll find something."

He made himself glance at her. The sunset burned on the willow leaves above and on her face, which was now turned toward the infant he could not see. "Come back to Nakamura," he said.

"No. Anywhere else."

"You always loved the mountains," he groped. "We—"

"No." She met his eyes. "It isn't you, Dad. Never you. But Jimmy is not going to grow up a soldier." She hesitated. "I'm sure some of the Espers will keep going, on a new basis, but with the same goals. I think we should join them. He ought to believe in something different from what killed his father, and work for it to become real. Don't you agree?"

Mackenzie climbed to his feet against Earth's hard pull. "I don't know," he said. "Never was a thinker . . . Can I see him?"

"Oh, Dad—"

He went over and looked down at the small sleeping form. "If you marry again," he said, "and have a daughter, would you call her for her mother?" He saw Laura's head bend downward and her hands clench. Quickly he said, "I'll go now. I'd like to visit you some more, tomorrow or sometime, if you'll have me."

Then she came to his arms and wept. He stroked her hair and murmured, as he had done when she was a child. "You do want to return to the mountains, don't you? They're your country too, your people, where you belong."

"Y-you'll never know how much I want to."

"Then why not?" he cried.

His daughter straightened herself. "I can't," she said. "Your war is ended. Mine has just begun."

Because he had trained that will, he could only say, "I hope you win it."

"Perhaps in a thousand years—" She could not continue.

Night had fallen when he left her. Power

was still out in the city, so the street lamps were dark and the stars stood forth above all roofs. The squad that waited to accompany their colonel to barracks looked wolfish by lantern light. They saluted him and rode at his back, rifles ready for trouble; but there was only the iron sound of horseshoes.

GREG BEAR

☐ 53172-8   BEYOND HEAVEN'S RIVER $2.95
☐ 53173-6   Canada $3.95

☐ 53174-4   EON $3.95
☐ 53175-2   Canada $4.95

☐ 53167-1   THE FORGE OF GOD $4.50
☐ 53168-X   Canada $5.50

☐ 55971-1   HARDFOUGHT (Tor Double with
                Cascade Point by Timothy Zahn $2.95
☐ 55951-7   Canada $3.95

☐ 53163-9   HEGIRA $3.95
☐ 53164-7   Canada $4.95

☐ 53165-5   PSYCHLONE $3.95
☐ 53166-3   Canada $4.95

"RESSPECTFFUL GREETINGSS, SSIR," THE CAT HISSED. "NAME IZZ KIM."

Doc answered, "The same to you, sir. May mice be ever abundant." He softly stroked the cat, beginning with Kim's chin and chest. The dreaminess returned to his voice. "In the Old Days, all cats talked, not just a few sports. The entire feline tribe. And many dogs, too—pardon me, Kim. While as for dolphins and whales and apes . . ."

Spar said eagerly, "Answer me one question, Doc. If your pills give happiness without hangover, why do you always drink moonbrew yourself and sometimes spike it with moonmist?"

"Because for me—" Doc began and then broke it off with a grin. "You've trapped me, Spar. I never thought you used your mind. Very well, on your own mind be it."

From under Spar's chin, Kim hissed very softly, but urgently, "Sstop! Ssilence, on your liffe!" Spar was getting used to Kim's melodrama.

The Tor Double Novels

*forthcoming

FRITZ LEIBER
SHIP OF SHADOWS

A TOM DOHERTY ASSOCIATES BOOK
NEW YORK

SHIP OF SHADOWS

Copyright © 1969 by Mercury Press, Inc.

Reprinted by permission of the author and his agent, Richard Curtis Associates, Inc.

A TOR Book
Published by Tom Doherty Associates, Inc.
49 West 24 Street
New York, NY 10010

Cover art by Robin Wood

ISBN: 0-812-55958-4   Can. ISBN: 0-812-55954-1

First Tor edition: February 1989

Printed in the United States of America

0 9 8 7 6 5 4 3 2 1

"**I**SSIOT! Ffffool! Lushshsh!" hissed the cat and bit Spar somewhere.

The fourfold sting of the eye teeth balanced the gut-wretchedness of his looming hangover, so that Spar's mind floated as free as his body in the blackness of Windrush, in which shone only a couple of running lights dim as churning dream-glow and infinitely distant as the Bridge or the Stern.

The vision came of a ship with all sails set creaming through blue, wind-ruffled sea against a blue sky. The last two nouns were not obscene now. He could hear the whistle of the salty wind through shrouds and stays, its drumming against the taut sails, and the creak of the three masts and all the rest of the ship's wood.

What was wood? From somewhere came the answer: plastic alive-o.

And what force flattened the water and kept it from breaking up into great globules and the ship from spinning away, keel over masts, in the wind?

1

Instead of being blurred and rounded like reality, the vision was sharp-edged and bright —the sort Spar never told, for fear of being accused of second sight and so of witchcraft.

Windrush was a ship too, was often called the Ship. But it was a strange sort of ship, in which the sailors lived forever in the shrouds inside cabins of all shapes made of translucent sails welded together. And it was a ship that was not sailing anywhere, because it had everywhere in it—it was all there was.

The only other things the two ships shared were the wind and the unending creaking. As the vision faded, Spar began to hear the winds of Windrush softly moaning through the long passageways, while he felt the creaking in the vibrant shroud to which he was clipped wrist and ankle to keep him from floating around in the Bat Rack.

Sleepday's dreams had begun good, with Spar having Crown's three girls at once. But Sleepday night he had been half-waked by the distant grinding of Hold Three's big chewer. Then werewolves and vampires had attacked him, solid shadows diving in from all six corners, while witches and their familiars tittered in the black shadowy background. Somehow he had been protected by the cat, familiar of a slim witch whose bared teeth had been an ivory blur in the larger silver blur of her wild hair. Spar pressed his rubbery gums together. The cat had been the last of the supernatural

2

creatures to fade. Then had come the beautiful vision of the ship.

His hangover hit him suddenly and mercilessly. Sweat shook off him until he must be surrounded by a cloud of it. Without warning his gut reversed. His free hand found a floating waste tube in time to press its small trumpet to his face. He could hear his acrid vomit gurgling away, urged by a light suction.

His gut reversed again, quick as the flap of a safety hatch when a gale blows up in the corridors. He thrust the waste tube inside the leg of his short, loose slopsuit and caught the dark stuff, almost as watery and quite as explosive as his vomit. Then he had the burning urge to make water.

Afterwards, feeling blessedly weak, Spar curled up in the equally blessed dark and prepared to snooze until Keeper woke him.

"Sssot!" hissed the cat. "Sssleep no more! Sssee! Sssee shshsharply!"

In his left shoulder, through the worn fabric of his slopsuit, Spar could feel four sets of prickles, like the touch of small thorn clusters in the Gardens of Apollo or Diana. He froze.

"Sspar," the cat hissed more softly, quitting to prickle. "I wishsh you all besst. Mosst ashshuredly."

Spar warily reached his right hand across his chest, touched short fur softer than Suzy's, and stroked gingerly.

The cat hissed very softly, almost purring,

3

"Ssturdy Sspar! Ssee ffar! Ssee fforever! Fforessee! Afftssee!"

Spar felt a surge of irritation at this constant talk of seeing—bad manners in the cat!—followed by an irrational surge of hope about his eyes. He decided that this was no witch cat left over from his dream, but a stray which had wormed its way through a wind tube into the Bat Rack, setting off his dream. There were quite a few animal strays in these days of the witch panic and the depopulation of the Ship, or at least of Hold Three.

Dawn struck the Bow then, for the violet fore-corner of the Bat Rack began to glow. The running lights were drowned in a growing white blaze. Within twenty heartbeats Windrush was bright as it ever would be on Workday or any other morning.

Out along Spar's arm moved the cat, a black blur to his squinting eyes. In teeth Spar could not see, it held a smaller gray blur. Spar touched the latter. It was even shorter furred, but cold.

As if irked, the cat took off from his bare forearm with a strong push of hind legs. It landed expertly on the next shroud, a wavery line of gray that vanished in either direction before reaching a wall.

Spar unclipped himself, curled his toes round his own pencil-thin shroud, and squinted at the cat.

The cat stared back with eyes that were

4

green blurs which almost coalesced in the black blur of its outsize head.

Spar asked, "Your child? Dead?"

The cat loosed its gray burden, which floated beside its head.

"Chchchchild!" All the former scorn and more were back in the sibilant voice. "It izzzz a rat I sssslew her, issssiot!"

Spar's lips puckered in a smile. "I like you, cat. I will call you Kim."

"Kim-shlim!" the cat spat. "I'll call you Lushshsh! Or Sssot!"

The creaking increased, as it always did after dayspring and noon. Shrouds twanged. Walls crackled.

Spar swiftly swiveled his head. Though reality was by its nature a blur, he could unerringly spot movement.

Keeper was slowly floating straight at him. On the round of his russet body was mounted the great, pale round of his face, its bright pink target-center drawing attention from the tiny, wide-set, brown blurs of his eyes. One of his fat arms ended in the bright gleam of pliofilm, the other in the dark gleam of steel. Far beyond him was the dark red aft corner of the Bat Rack, with the great gleaming torus, or doughnut, of the bar midway between.

"Lazy, pampered he-slut," Keeper greeted. "All Sleepday you snored while I stood guard, and now I bring your morning pouch of moonmist to your sleeping shroud.

"A bad night, Spar," he went on, his voice growing sententious. "Werewolves, vampires, and witches loose in the corridors. But I stood them off, not to mention rats and mice. I heard through the tubes that the vamps got Girlie and Sweetheart, the silly sluts! Vigilance, Spar! Now suck your moonmist and start sweeping. The place stinks."

He stretched out the pliofilm-gleaming hand.

His mind hissing with Kim's contemptuous words, Spar said, "I don't think I'll drink this morning, Keeper. Corn gruel and moonbrew only. No, water."

"What, Spar?" Keeper demanded. "I don't believe I can allow that. We don't want you having convulsions in front of the customers. Earth strangle me!—what's that?"

Spar instantly launched himself at Keeper's steel-gleaming hand. Behind him his shroud twanged. With one hand he twisted a cold, thick barrel. With the other he pried a plump finger from a trigger.

"He's not a witch cat, only a stray," he said as they tumbled over and kept slowly rotating.

"Unhand me, underling!" Keeper blustered. "I'll have you in irons. I'll tell Crown."

"Shooting weapons are as much against the law as knives or needles," Spar countered boldly, though he already was feeling dizzy and sick. "It's you should fear the brig." He recognized beneath the bullying voice the awe

Keeper always had of his ability to move swiftly and surely, though half-blind.

They bounced to rest against a swarm of shrouds. "Loose me, I say," Keeper demanded, struggling weakly. "Crown gave me this pistol. And I have a permit for it from the Bridge." The last at least, Spar guessed, was a lie. Keeper continued, "Besides, it's only a line-shooting gun reworked for heavy, elastic ball. Not enough to rupture a wall, yet sufficient to knock out drunks—or knock in the head of a witch cat!"

"Not a witch cat, Keeper," Spar repeated, although he was having to swallow hard to keep from spewing. "Only a well-behaved stray, who has already proved his use to us by killing one of the rats that have been stealing our food. His name is Kim. He'll be a good worker."

The distant blur of Kim lengthened and showed thin blurs of legs and tail, as if he were standing out rampant from his line. "Assset izz I," he boasted. "Ssanitary. Uzze wasste tubes. Sslay ratss, micece! Sspy out witchchess, vampss ffor you!"

"He speaks!" Keeper gasped. "Witchcraft!"

"Crown has a dog who talks," Spar answered with finality. "A talking animal's no proof of anything."

All this while he had kept firm hold of barrel and finger. Now he felt through their grappled bodies a change in Keeper, as though inside

7

his blubber the master of the Bat Rack were transforming from stocky muscle and bone into a very thick, sweet syrup that could conform to and flow around anything.

"Sorry, Spar," he whispered unctuously. "It was a bad night and Kim startled me. He's black like a witch cat. An easy mistake on my part. We'll try him out at catcher. He must earn his keep! Now take your drink."

The pliant double pouch filling Spar's palm felt like the philosopher's stone. He lifted it toward his lips, but at the same time his toes unwittingly found a shroud, and he dove swiftly toward the shining torus, which had a hole big enough to accommodate four barmen at a pinch.

Spar collapsed against the opposite inside of the hole. With a straining of its shrouds, the torus absorbed his impact. He had the pouch to his lips, its cap unscrewed, but had not squeezed. He shut his eyes and with a tiny sob blindly thrust the pouch back into the moonmist cage.

Working chiefly by touch, he took a pouch of corn gruel from the hot closet, snitching at the same time a pouch of coffee and thrusting it into an inside pocket. Then he took a pouch of water, opened it, shoved in five salt tablets, closed it, and shook and squeezed it vigorously.

Keeper, having drifted behind him, said into his ear, "So you drink anyhow. Moonmist not good enough, you make yourself a cocktail.

8

I should dock it from your scrip. But all drunks are liars, or become so."

Unable to ignore the taunt, Spar explained, "No, only salt water to harden my gums."

"Poor Spar, what'll you ever need hard gums for? Planning to share rats with your new friend? Don't let me catch you roasting them in my grill! I should dock you for the salt. To sweeping, Spar!" Then turning his head toward the violet fore-corner and speaking loudly, "And you! Catch mice!"

Kim had already found the small chewer tube and thrust the dead rat into it, gripping tube with foreclaws and pushing rat with aft. At the touch of the rat's cadaver against the solid wrist of the tube, a grinding began there which would continue until the rat was macerated and slowly swallowed away toward the great cloaca which fed the Gardens of Diana.

Three times Spar manfully swished salt water against his gums and spat into a waste tube, vomiting a little after the first gargle. Then facing away from Keeper as he gently squeezed the pouches, he forced into his throat the coffee—dearer than moonmist, the drink distilled from moonbrew—and some of the corn gruel.

He apologetically offered the rest to Kim, who shook his head. "Jusst had a mousse."

Hastily Spar made his way to the green starboard corner. Outside the hatch he heard some drunks calling with weary and mournful anger, "Unzip!"

Grasping the heads of two long waste tubes, Spar began to sweep the air, working out from the green corner in a spiral, quite like an orb spider building her web.

From the torus, where he was idly polishing its thin titanium, Keeper upped the suction on the two tubes, so that reaction sped Spar in his spiral. He need use his body only to steer course and to avoid shrouds in such a way that his tubes didn't tangle.

Soon Keeper glanced at his wrist and called, "Spar, can't you keep track of the time? Open up!" He threw a ring of keys which Spar caught, though he could see only the last half of their flight. As soon as he was well headed toward the green door, Keeper called again and pointed aft and aloft. Spar obediently unlocked and unzipped the dark and also the blue hatch, though there was no one at either, before opening the green. In each case he avoided the hatch's gummy margin and the sticky emergency hatch hinged close beside.

In tumbled three brewos, old customers, snatching at shrouds and pushing off from each other's bodies in their haste to reach the torus, and meanwhile cursing Spar.

"Sky strangle you!"

"Earth bury you!"

"Seas sear you!"

"Language, boys!" Keeper reproved. "Though I'll agree my helper's stupidity and sloth tempt a man to talk foul."

Spar threw the keys back. The brewos lined up elbow to elbow around the torus, three grayish blobs with heads pointing toward the blue corner.

Keeper faced them. "Below, below!" he ordered indignantly. "You think you're gents?"

"But you're serving no one aloft yet."

"There's only us three."

"No matter," Keeper replied. "Propriety, suckers! Unless you mean to buy by the pouch, invert."

With low grumbles the brewos reversed their bodies so that their heads pointed toward the black corner.

Himself not bothering to invert, Keeper tossed them a slim and twisty faint red blur with three branches. Each grabbed a branch and stuck it in his face.

The pudge of his fat hand on glint of valve, Keeper said, "Let's see your scrip first."

With angry mumbles each unwadded something too small for Spar to see clearly, and handed it over. Keeper studied each item before feeding it to the cashbox. Then he decreed, "Six seconds of moonbrew. Suck fast," and looked at his wrist and moved the other hand.

One of the brewos seemed to be strangling, but he blew out through his nose and kept sucking bravely.

Keeper closed the valve.

Instantly one brewo splutteringly accused, "You cut us off too soon. That wasn't six."

The treacle back in his voice, Keeper explained, "I'm squirting it to you four and two. Don't want you to drown. Ready again?"

The brewos greedily took their second squirt and then, at times wistfully sucking their tubes for remnant drops, began to shoot the breeze. In his distant circling, Spar's keen ears heard most of it.

"A dirty Sleepday, Keeper."

"No, a good one, brewo—for a drunken sucker to get his blood sucked by a lust-tickling vamp."

"I was dossed safe at Pete's, you fat ghoul."

"Pete's safe? That's news!"

"Dirty Atoms to you! But vamps did get Girlie and Sweetheart. Right in the starboard main drag, if you can believe it. By Cobalt Ninety, Windrush is getting lonely! Third Hold, anyhow. You can swim a whole passageway by day without meeting a soul."

"How do you know that about the girls?" the second brewo demanded. "Maybe they've gone to another hold to change their luck."

"Their luck's run out. Suzy saw them snatched."

"Not Suzy," Keeper corrected, now playing umpire. "But Mabel did. A proper fate for drunken sluts."

"You've got no heart, Keeper."

"True enough. That's why the vamps pass

me by. But speaking serious, boys, the werethings and witches are running too free in Three. I was awake all Sleepday guarding. I'm sending a complaint to the Bridge."

"You're kidding."

"You wouldn't."

Keeper solemnly nodded his head and crossed his left chest. The brewos were impressed.

Spar spiraled back toward the green corner, sweeping farther from the wall. On his way he overtook the black blob of Kim, who was circling the periphery himself, industriously leaping from shroud to shroud and occasionally making dashes along them.

A fair-skinned, plump shape twice circled by blue—bra and culottes—swam in through the green hatch.

"Morning, Spar," a soft voice greeted. "How's it going?"

"Fair and foul," Spar replied. The golden cloud of blonde hair floating loose touched his face. "I'm quitting moonmist, Suzy."

"Don't be too hard on yourself, Spar. Work a day, loaf a day, play a day, sleep a day—that way it's best."

"I know. Workday, Loafday, Playday, Sleepday. Ten days make a terranth, twelve terranths make a sunth, twelve sunths make a starth, and so on, to the end of time. With corrections, some tell me. I wish I knew what all those names mean."

"You're too serious. You should— Oh, a kitten! How darling!"

"Kitten-shmitten!" the big-headed black blur hissed as it leapt past them. "Izzz cat. IZZZ Kim."

"Kim's our new catcher," Spar explained. "He's serious too."

"Quit wasting time on old Toothless Eyeless, Suzy," Keeper called, "and come all the way in."

As Suzy complied with a sigh, taking the easy route of the ratlines, her soft taper fingers brushed Spar's crumpled cheek. "Dear Spar . . ." she murmured. As her feet passed his face, there was a jingle of her charm-anklet—all gold-washed hearts, Spar knew.

"Hear about Girlie and Sweetheart?" a brewo greeted ghoulishly. "How'd you like your carotid or outside iliac sliced, your—?"

"Shut up, sucker!" Suzy wearily cut him off. "Gimme a drink, Keeper."

"Your tab's long, Suzy. How you going to pay?"

"Don't play games, Keeper, please. Not in the morning, anyhow. You know all the answers, especially to that one. For now, a pouch of moonbrew, dark. And a little quiet."

"Pouches are for ladies, Suzy. I'll serve you aloft, you got to meet your marks, but—"

There was a shrill snarl which swiftly mounted to a scream of rage. Just inside the aft hatch, a pale figure in vermilion culottes and

bra—no, wider than that, jacket or short coat—was struggling madly, somersaulting and kicking.

Entering carelessly, likely too swiftly, the slim girl had got parts of herself and her clothes stuck to the hatch's inside margin and the emergency hatch.

Breaking loose by frantic main force while Spar dove toward her and the brewos shouted advice, she streaked toward the torus, jerking at the ratlines, black hair streaming behind her.

Coming up with a *bong* of hip against titanium, she grabbed together her vermilion—yes, clutch coat with one hand and thrust the other across the rocking bar.

Drifting in close behind, Spar heard her say, "Double pouch of moonmist, Keeper. Make it fast."

"The best of mornings to you, Rixende," Keeper greeted. "I would gladly serve you goldwater, except, well—" The fat arms spread "—Crown doesn't like his girls coming to the Bat Rack by themselves. Last time he gave me strict orders to—"

"What the smoke! It's on Crown's account I came here, to find something he lost. Meanwhile, moonmist. Double!" She pounded on the bar until reaction started her aloft, and she pulled back into place with Spar's unthanked help.

"Softly, softly, lady," Keeper gentled, the

tiny brown blurs of his eyes vanishing with his grinning. "What if Crown comes in while you're squeezing?"

"He won't!" Rixende denied vehemently, though glancing past Spar quickly—black blur, blur of pale face, black blur again. "He's got a new girl. I don't mean Phanette or Doucette, but a girl you've never seen. Name of Almodie. He'll be busy with the skinny bitch all morning. And now uncage that double moonmist, you dirty devil!"

"Softly, Rixie. All in good time. What is it Crown lost?"

"A little black bag. About so big." She extended her slender hand, fingers merged. "He lost it here last Playday night, or had it lifted."

"Hear that, Spar?" Keeper said.

"No little black bags," Spar said very quickly. "But you did leave your big orange one here last night, Rixende. I'll get it." He swung inside the torus.

"Oh, damn both bags. Gimme that double!" the black-haired girl demanded frantically. "Earth Mother!"

Even the brewos gasped. Touching hands to the side of his head, Keeper begged. "No big obscenities, please. They sound worse from a dainty girl, gentle Rixende."

"Earth Mother, I said! Now cut the fancy, Keeper, and give, before I scratch your face off and rummage your cages!"

"Very well, very well. At once, at once. But how will you pay? Crown told me he'd get my license revoked if I ever put you on his tab again. Have you scrip? Or . . . coins?"

"Use your eyes! Or you think this coat's got inside pockets?" She spread it wide, flashing her upper body, then clutched it tight again. "Earth Mother! Earth Mother! Earth Mother!" The brewos babbled scandalized. Suzy snorted mildly in boredom.

With one fat hand-blob Keeper touched Rixende's wrist where a yellow blur circled it closely. "You've got gold," he said in hushed tones, his eyes vanishing again, this time in greed.

"You know damn well they're welded on. My anklets too."

"But these?" His hand went to a golden blur close beside her head.

"Welded too. Crown had my ears pierced."

"But . . ."

"Oh, you atom-dirty devil! I get you, all right. Well, then, *all right!*" The last words ended in a scream more of anger than pain as she grabbed a gold blur and jerked. Blood swiftly blobbed out. She thrust forward her fisted hand. "Now *give!* Gold for a double moonmist."

Keeper breathed hard but said nothing as he scrabbled in the moonmist cage, as if knowing he had gone too far. The brewos were silent too. Suzy sounded completely unimpressed as

17

she said, "*And* my dark." Spar found a fresh dry sponge and expertly caught up the floating scarlet blobs with it before pressing it to Rixende's torn ear.

Keeper studied the heavy gold pendant, which he held close to his face. Rixende milked the double pouch pressed to her lips and her eyes vanished as she sucked blissfully. Spar guided Rixende's free hand to the sponge, and she automatically took over the task of holding it to her ear. Suzy gave a hopeless sigh, then reached her whole plump body across the bar, dipped her hand into a cool cage, and helped herself to a double of dark.

A long, wiry, very dark brown figure in skintight dark violet jumpers mottled with silver arrowed in from the dark red hatch at a speed half again as great as Spar ever dared and without brushing a single shroud by accident or intent. Midway the newcomer did a half somersault as he passed Spar, his long, narrow bare feet hit the titanium next to Rixende. He accordioned up so expertly that the torus hardly swayed.

One very dark brown arm snaked around her. The other plucked the pouch from her mouth, and there was a snap as he spun the cap shut.

A lazy musical voice inquired, "What'd we tell you would happen, baby, if you ever again took a drink on your own?"

The Bat Rack held very still. Keeper was backed against the opposite side of the hole, one hand behind him. Spar had his arm in his lost-and-found nook behind the moonbrew and moonmist cages and kept it there. He felt fear-sweat beading on him. Suzy kept her dark close to her face.

A brewo burst into violent coughing, choked it to a wheezing end, and gasped subserviently, "Excuse me, coroner. Salutations."

Keeper chimed dully, "Morning . . . Crown."

Crown gently pulled the clutch coat off Rixende's far shoulder and began to stroke her. "Why, you're all gooseflesh, honey, and rigid as a corpse. What frightened you? Smooth down, skin. Ease up, muscles. Relax, Rix, and we'll give you a squirt."

His hand found the sponge, stopped, investigated, found the wet part, then went toward the middle of his face. He sniffed.

"Well, boys, at least we know none of you are vamps," he observed softly. "Else we'd found you sucking at her ear."

Rixende said very rapidly in a monotone, "I didn't come for a drink, I swear to you. I came to get that little bag you lost. Then I was tempted. I didn't know I would be. I tried to resist, but Keeper led me on. I—"

"Shut up," Crown said quietly. "We were just wondering how you paid him. Now we know. How were you planning to buy your

third double? Cut off a hand or a foot? Keeper
. . . show me your other hand. We said show
it. That's right. Now unfist."

Crown plucked the pendant from Keeper's
opened hand-blob. His yellow-brown eye-
blurs on Keeper all the while, he wagged the
precious bauble back and forth, then tossed it
slowly aloft.

As the golden blur moved toward the open
blue hatch at unchanging pace, Keeper
opened and shut his mouth twice, then babbled, "I didn't tempt her, Crown, honest I
didn't. I didn't know she was going to hurt her
ear. I tried to stop her, but—"

"We're not interested," Crown said. "Put
the double on our tab." His face never leaving
Keeper's, he extended his arm aloft and
pinched the pendant just before it straight-
lined out of reach.

"Why's this home of jollity so dead?" Snak-
ing a long leg across the bar as easily as an arm,
Crown pinched Spar's ear between his big and
smaller toes, pulled him close and turned him
round. "How're you coming along with the
saline, baby? Gums hardening? Only one way
to test it." Gripping Spar's jaw and lip with his
other toes, he thrust the big one into Spar's
mouth. "Come on, bite me, baby."

Spar bit. It was the only way not to vomit.
Crown chuckled. Spar bit hard. Energy
flooded his shaking frame. His face grew hot

and his forehead throbbed under its drenching of fear-sweat. He was sure he was hurting Crown, but the Coroner of Hold Three only kept up his low, delighted chuckle and when Spar gasped, withdrew his foot.

"My, my, you're getting strong, baby. We almost felt that. Have a drink on us."

Spar ducked his stupidly wide-open mouth away from the thin jet of moonmist. The jet struck him in his eye and stung so that he had to knot his fists and clamp his aching gums together to keep from crying out.

"Why's this place so dead, I ask again? No applause for baby and now baby's gone temperance on us. Can't you give us just one tiny laugh?" Crown faced each in turn. "What's the matter? Cat got your tongues?"

"Cat? We have a cat, a new cat, came just last night, working as catcher," Keeper suddenly babbled. "It can talk a little. Not as well as Hellhound, but it talks. It's very funny. It caught a rat."

"What'd you do with the rat's body, Keeper?"

"Fed it to the chewer. That is, Spar did. Or the cat."

"You mean to tell us that you disposed of a corpse without notifying us? Oh, don't go pale on us, Keeper. That's nothing. Why, we could accuse you of harboring a witch cat. You say he came last night, and that was a wicked night

for witches. Now don't go green on us too. We were only putting you on. We were only looking for a small laugh."

"Spar! Call your cat! Make him say something funny."

Before Spar could call, or even decide whether he'd call Kim or not, the black blur appeared on a shroud near Crown, green eye-blurs fixed on the yellow-brown ones.

"So you're the joker, eh? Well . . . joke."

Kim increased in size. Spar realized it was his fur standing on end.

"Go ahead, joke . . . like they tell us you can. Keeper, you wouldn't be kidding us about this cat being able to talk?"

"Spar! Make your cat joke!"

"Don't bother. We believe he's got his own tongue too. That the matter, Blackie?" He reached out his hand. Kim lashed at it and sprang away. Crown only gave another of his low chuckles.

Rixende began to shake uncontrollably. Crown examined her solicitously yet leisurely, using his outstretched hand to turn her head toward him, so that any blood that might have been coming from it from the cat's slash would have gone into the sponge.

"Spar swore the cat could talk," Keeper babbled. "I'll—"

"Quiet," Crown said. He put the pouch to Rixende's lips, squeezed until her shaking

subsided and it was empty, then flicked the crumpled pliofilm toward Spar.

"And now about that little black bag, Keeper," Crown said flatly.

"Spar!"

The latter dipped into his lost-and-found nook, saying quickly, "No little black bags, coroner, but we did find this one the lady Rixende forgot last Playday night," and he turned back holding out something big, round, gleamingly orange, and closed with draw strings.

Crown took and swung it slowly in a circle. For Spar, who couldn't see the strings, it was like magic. "Bit too big, and a mite the wrong shade. We're certain we lost the little black bag here, or had it lifted. You making the Bat Rack a tent for dips, Keeper?"

"Spar—?"

"We're asking *you*, Keeper."

Shoving Spar aside, Keeper groped frantically in the nook, pulling aside the cages of moonmist and moonbrew pouches. He produced many small objects. Spar could distinguish the largest—an electric hand-fan and a bright red footglove. They hung around Keeper in a jumble.

Keeper was panting and had scrabbled his hands for a full minute in the nook without bringing out anything more, when Crown said, his voice lazy again, "That's enough. The little

black bag was of no importance to us in any case."

Keeper emerged with a face doubly blurred. It must be surrounded by a haze of sweat. He pointed an arm at the orange bag.

"It might be inside that one!"

Crown opened the bag, began to search through it, changed his mind, and gave the whole bag a flick. Its remarkably numerous contents came out and moved slowly aloft at equal speeds, like an army on the march in irregular order. Crown scanned them as they went past.

"No, not there." He pushed the bag toward Keeper. "Return Rix's stuff to it and have it ready for us the next time we dive in—"

Putting his arm around Rixende, so that it was his hand that held the sponge to her ear, he turned and kicked off powerfully for the aft hatch. After he had been out of sight for several seconds, there was a general sigh, the three brewos put out new scrip-wads to pay for another squirt. Suzy asked for a second double dark, which Spar handed her quickly, while Keeper shook off his daze and ordered Spar, "Gather up all the floating trash, especially Rixie's, and get that back in her purse. On the jump, lubber!" Then he used the electric hand-fan to cool and dry himself.

It was a mean task Keeper had set Spar, but Kim came to help, darting after objects too small for Spar to see. Once he had them in his

hands, Spar could readily finger or sniff which was which.

When his impotent rage at Crown had faded, Spar's thoughts went back to Sleepday night. Had his vision of vamps and werewolves been dream only?—now that he knew the werethings had been abroad in force. If only he had better eyes to distinguish illusion from reality! Kim's "Sssee! Sssee shshsharply!" hissed in his memory. What would it be like to see sharply? Everything brighter? Or closer?

After a weary time the scattered objects were gathered and he went back to sweeping and Kim to his mouse hunt. As Workday morning progressed, the Bat Rack gradually grew less bright, though so gradually it was hard to tell.

A few more customers came in, but all for quick drinks, which Keeper served them glumly; Suzy judged none of them worth cottoning up to.

As time slowly passed, Keeper grew steadily more fretfully angry, as Spar had known he would after groveling before Crown. He tried to throw out the three brewos, but they produced more crumpled scrip, which closest scrutiny couldn't prove counterfeit. In revenge he short-squirted them and there were arguments. He called Spar off his sweeping to ask him nervously, "That cat of yours—he scratched Crown, didn't he? We'll have to get rid of him; Crown said he might be a witch cat,

remember?" Spar made no answer. Keeper set him renewing the glue of the emergency hatches, claiming that Rixende's tearing free from the aft one had shown it must be drying out. He gobbled appetizers and drank moonmist with tomato juice. He sprayed the Bat Rack with some abominable synthetic scent. He started counting the boxed scrip and coins but gave up the job with a slam of self-locking drawer almost before he'd begun. His grimace fixed on Suzy.

"Spar!" he called. "Take over! And over-squirt the brewos on your peril!"

Then he locked the cash box, and giving Suzy a meaningful jerk of his head toward the scarlet starboard hatch, he pulled himself toward it. With an unhappy shrug toward Spar, she wearily followed.

As soon as the pair were gone, Spar gave the brewos an eight-second squirt, waving back their scrip, and placed two small serving cages —of fritos and yeast balls—before them. They grunted their thanks and fell to. The light changed from healthy bright to corpse white. There was a faint, distant roar, followed some seconds later by a brief crescendo of creakings. The new light made Spar uneasy. He served two more suck-and-dives and sold a pouch of moonmist at double purser's prices. He started to eat an appetizer, but just then Kim swam in to show him proudly a mouse. He

conquered his nausea, but began to dread the onset of real withdrawal symptoms.

A pot-bellied figure clad in sober black dragged itself along the ratlines from the green hatch. On the aloft side of the bar there appeared a visage in which the blur of white hair and beard almost hid leather-brown flesh, though accentuating the blurs of gray eyes.

"Doc!" Spar greeted, his misery and unease gone, and instantly handed out a chill pouch of three-star moonbrew. Yet all he could think to say in his excitement was the banal, "A bad Sleepday night, eh, Doc? Vamps and—"

"—And other doltish superstitions, which wax every sunth, but never wane," an amiable, cynical old voice cut in. "Yet, I suppose I shouldn't rob you of your illusions, Spar, even the terrifying ones. You've little enough to live by, as it is. And there *is* viciousness astir in Windrush. Ah, that smacks good against my tonsils."

Then Spar remembered the important thing. Reaching deep inside his slopsuit, he brought out, in such a way as to hide it from the brewos below, a small flat narrow black bag.

"Here, Doc," he whispered, "you lost it last Playday. I kept it safe for you."

"Dammit, I'd lose my jumpers, if I ever took them off," Doc commented, hushing his voice when Spar put finger to lips. "I suppose I

started mixing moonmist with my moonbrew
—again?"

"You did, Doc. But you didn't lose your bag.
Crown or one of his girls lifted it, or snagged it
when it sat loose beside you. And then I . . . I,
Doc, lifted it from Crown's hip pocket. Yes,
and kept that secret when Rixende and Crown
came in demanding it this morning."

"Spar, my boy, I am deeply in your debt,"
Doc said. "More than you can know. Another
three-star, please. Ah, nectar. Spar, ask any
reward of me, and if it lies merely within the
realm of the first transfinite infinity, I will
grant it."

To his own surprise, Spar began to shake—
with excitement. Pulling himself forward halfway across the bar, he whispered hoarsely,
"Give me good eyes, Doc!" adding impulsively, "and teeth!"

After what seemed a long while, Doc said in
a dreamy, sorrowful voice, "In the Old Days,
that would have been easy. They'd perfected
eye transplants. They could regenerate cranial
nerves, and sometimes restore scanning power
to an injured cerebrum. While transplanting
tooth buds from a stillborn was intern's play.
But now . . . Oh, I might be able to do what
you ask in an uncomfortable, antique, inorgan-
ic fashion, but . . ." He broke off on a note that
spoke of the misery of life and the uselessness
of all effort.

"The Old Days," one brewo said from the

corner of his mouth to the brewo next to him. "Witch talk!"

"Witch-smitch!" the second brewo replied in like fashion. "The flesh mechanic's only senile. He dreams all four days, not just Sleepday."

The third brewo whistled against the evil eye a tune like the wind.

Spar tugged at the long-armed sleeve of Doc's black jumper. "Doc, you promised. I want to see sharp, bite sharp!"

Doc laid his shrunken hand commiseratingly on Spar's forearm. "Spar," he said softly, "seeing sharply would only make you very unhappy. Believe me, I *know*. Life's easier to bear when things are blurred, just as it's best when thoughts are blurred by brew or mist. And while there are people in Windrush who yearn to bite sharply, you are not their kind. Another three-star, if you please."

"I quit moonmist this morning, Doc," Spar said somewhat proudly as he handed over the fresh pouch.

Doc answered with sad smile, "Many quit moonmist every Workday morning and change their minds when Playday comes around."

"Not me, Doc! Besides," Spar argued, "Keeper and Crown and his girls and even Suzy all see sharply, and they aren't unhappy."

"I'll tell you a secret, Spar," Doc replied. "Keeper and Crown and the girls are all

zombies. Yes, even Crown with his cunning and power. To them Windrush is the universe."

"It isn't, Doc?"

Ignoring the interruption, Doc continued, "But you wouldn't be like that, Spar. You'd want to know more. And that would make you far unhappier than you are."

"I don't care, Doc," Spar said. He repeated accusingly, "You promised."

The gray blurs of Doc's eyes almost vanished as he frowned in thought. Then he said, "How would this be, Spar? I know moonmist brings pains and sufferings as well as easings and joys. But suppose that every Workday morning and Loafday noon I should bring you a tiny pill that would give you all the good effects of moonmist and none of the bad. I've one in this bag. Try it now and see. And every Playday night I would bring you without fail another sort of pill that would make you sleep soundly with never a nightmare. Much better than eyes and teeth. Think it over."

As Spar considered that, Kim drifted up. He eyed Doc with his close-set green blurs. "Resspectfful greetingss, ssir," he hissed. "Name izz Kim."

Doc answered, "The same to you, sir. May mice be ever abundant." He softly stroked the cat, beginning with Kim's chin and chest. The

dreaminess returned to his voice. "In the Old Days, all cats talked, not just a few sports. The entire feline tribe. And many dogs, too—pardon me, Kim. While as for dolphins and whales and apes . . ."

Spar said eagerly, "Answer me one question, Doc. If your pills give happiness without hangover, why do you always drink moonbrew yourself and sometimes spike it with moonmist?"

"Because for me—" Doc began and then broke off with a grin. "You've trapped me, Spar. I never thought you used your mind. Very well, on your own mind be it. Come to my office this Loafday—you know the way? Good!—and we'll see what we can do about your eyes and teeth. And now a double pouch for the corridor."

He paid in bright coins, thrust the big squunchy three-star in a big pocket, said, "See you, Spar. So long, Kim," and tugged himself toward the green hatch, zig-zagging.

"Ffarewell, ssir," Kim hissed after him.

Spar held out the small black bag. "You forgot it again, Doc."

As Doc returned with a weary curse and pocketed it, the scarlet hatch unzipped and Keeper swam out. He looked in a good humor now and whistled the tune of "I'll Marry the Man on the Bridge" as he began to study certain rounds on scrip-till and moonbrew

valves, but when Doc was gone he asked Spar suspiciously, "What was that you handed the old geezer?"

"His purse," Spar replied easily. "He just forgot it now." He shook his loosely fisted hand and it chinked. "Doc paid in coins, Keeper." Keeper took them eagerly. "Back to sweeping, Spar."

As Spar dove toward the scarlet hatch to take up larboard tubes, Suzy emerged and passed him with face averted. She sidled up to the bar and unsmilingly snatched the pouch of moonmist Keeper offered her with mock courtliness.

Spar felt a brief rage on her behalf, but it was hard for him to keep his mind on anything but his coming appointment with Doc. When Workday night fell swiftly as a hurled knife, he was hardly aware of it and felt none of his customary unease. Keeper turned on full all of the lights in the Bat Rack. They shone brightly while beyond the translucent walls there was a milky churning.

Business picked up a little. Suzy made off with the first likely mark. Keeper called Spar to take over the torus, while he himself got a much-erased sheet of paper and holding it to a clipboard held against his bent knees, wrote on it laboriously, as if he were thinking out each word, perhaps each letter, often wetting his pencil in his mouth. He became so absorbed in his difficult task that without realiz-

ing he drifted off toward the black below hatch, rotating over and over. The paper got dirtier and dirtier with his scrawlings and smudgings, new erasures, saliva and sweat.

The short night passed more swiftly than Spar dared hope, so that the sudden glare of Loafday dawn startled him. Most of the customers made off to take their siestas.

Spar wondered what excuse to give Keeper for leaving the Bat Rack, but the problem was solved for him. Keeper folded the grimy sheet, and sealed it with hot tape. "Take this to the Bridge, loafer, to the Exec. Wait." He took the repacked, orange bag from its nook and pulled on the cords to make sure they were drawn tight. "On your way deliver this at Crown's Hole. With all courtesy and subservience, Spar! Now, on the jump!"

Spar slid the sealed message into his only pocket with working zipper and drew that tight. Then he dove slowly toward the aft hatch, where he almost collided with Kim. Recalling Keeper's talk of getting rid of the cat, he caught hold of him around the slim furry chest under the forelegs and gently thrust him inside his slopsuit, whispering, "You'll take a trip with me, little Kim." The cat set his claws in the thin material and steadied himself.

For Spar, the corridor was a narrow cylinder ending in mist either way and decorated by lengthwise blurs of green and red. He guided

himself chiefly by touch and memory, this time remembering that he must pull himself against the light wind hand-over-hand along the centerline. After curving past the larger cylinders of the fore-and-aft gangways, the corridor straightened. Twice he worked his way around centrally slung fans whirring so softly that he recognized them chiefly by the increase in breeze before passing them and the slight suction after.

Soon he began to smell soil and green stuff growing. With a shiver he passed a black round that was the elastic-curtained door to Hold Three's big chewer. He met no one— odd even for Loafday. Finally he saw the green of the Gardens of Apollo and beyond it a huge black screen, in which hovered toward the aft side a small, smoky-orange circle that always filled Spar with inexplicable sadness and fear. He wondered in how many black screens that doleful circle was portrayed, especially in the starboard end of Windrush. He had seen it in several.

So close to the gardens that he could make out wavering green shoots and the silhouette of a floating farmer, the corridor right-angled below. Two dozen pulls along the line and he floated by an open hatch, which both memory for distance and the strong scent of musky, mixed perfumes told him was the entry to Crown's Hole. Peering in, he could see the intermelting black and silver spirals of the

decor of the great globular room. Directly opposite the hatch was another large black screen with the red-mottled dun disk placed similarly off center.

From under Spar's chin, Kim hissed very softly, but urgently, "Sstop! Ssilencce, on your liffe!" The cat had poked his head out of the slopsuit's neck. His ears tickled Spar's throat. Spar was getting used to Kim's melodrama, and in any case the warning was hardly needed. He had just seen the half-dozen floating naked bodies and would have held still if only from embarrassment. Not that Spar could see genitals any more than ears at the distance. But he could see that save for hair, each body was of one texture: one very dark brown and the other five—or was it four? no, five—fair. He didn't recognize the two with platinum and golden hair, who also happened to be the two palest. He wondered which was Crown's new girl, name of Almodie. He was relieved that none of the bodies were touching.

There was the glint of metal by the golden-haired girl, and he could just discern the red blur of a slender, five-forked tube which went from the metal to the five other faces. It seemed strange that even with a girl to play bartender, Crown should have moonbrew served in such plebeian fashion in his palatial Hole. Of course the tube might carry moonwine, or even moonmist.

Or was Crown planning to open a rival bar

to the Bat Rack? A poor time, these days, and a worse location, he mused as he tried to think of what to do with the orange bag.

"Sslink offf!" Kim urged still more softly.

Spar's fingers found a snap-ring by the hatch. With the faintest of clicks he secured it around the draw-cords of the pouch and then pulled back the way he had come.

But faint as the click had been, there was a response from Crown's Hole—a very deep, long growl.

Spar pulled faster at the centerline. As he rounded the corner leading inboard, he looked back.

Jutting out from Crown's hatch was a big, prick-eared head narrower than a man's and darker even than Crown's.

The growl was repeated.

It was ridiculous he should be so frightened of Hellhound, Spar told himself as he jerked himself and his passenger along. Why, Crown sometimes even brought the big dog to the Bat Rack.

Perhaps it was that Hellhound never growled in the Bat Rack, only talked in a hundred or so monosyllables.

Besides, the dog couldn't pull himself along the centerline at any speed. He lacked sharp claws. Though he might be able to bound forward, caroming from one side of the corridor to another.

36

This time the center-slit black curtains of the big chewer made Spar veer violently. He was a fine one—going to get new eyes today and frightened as a child!

"Why did you try to scare me back there, Kim?" he asked angrily.

"I ssaw shsheer evil, isssiot!"

"You saw five folk sucking moonbrew. And a harmless dog. This time you're the fool, Kim, you're the idiot!"

Kim shut up, drawing in his head, and refused to say another word. Spar remembered about the vanity and touchiness of all cats. But by now he had other worries. What if the orange bag were stolen by a passerby before Crown noticed it? And if Crown did find it, wouldn't he know Spar, forever Keeper's errandboy, had been peeping? That all this should happen on the most important day of his life! His verbal victory over Kim was small consolation.

Also, although the platinum-haired girl had interested him most of the two strange ones, something began to bother him about the girl who'd been playing bartender, the one with golden hair like Suzy's, but much slimmer and paler—he had the feeling he'd seen her before. And something about her had frightened him.

When he reached the central gangways, he was tempted to go to Doc's office before the

Bridge. But he wanted to be able to relax at Doc's and take as much time as needed, knowing all errands were done.

Reluctantly he entered the windy violet gangway and dove at a fore angle for the first empty space on the central gang-line, so that his palms were only burned a little before he had firm hold of it and was being sped fore at about the same speed as the wind. Keeper was a miser, not to buy him handgloves, let alone footgloves!—but he had to pay sharp attention to passing the shroud-slung roller bearings that kept the thick, moving line centered in the big corridor. It was an easy trick to catch hold of the line ahead of the bearing and then get one's other hand out of the way, but it demanded watchfulness.

There were few figures traveling on the line and fewer still being blown along the corridor. He overtook a doubled up one tumbling over and over and crying out in an old cracked voice, "Jacob's Ladder, Tree of Life, Marriage Lines . . ."

He passed the squeeze in the gangway marking the division between the Third and Second Holds without being stopped by the guard there and then he almost missed the big blue corridor leading aloft. Again he slightly burned his palms making the transfer from one moving gang-line to another. His fretfulness increased.

"Sspar, you isssiot—!" Kim began.

"Ssh!—we're in officers' territory," Spar cut him off, glad to have that excuse for once more putting down the impudent cat. And true enough, the blue spaces of Windrush always did fill him with awe and dread.

Almost too soon to suit him, he found himself swinging from the gang-line to a stationary monkey jungle of tubular metal just below the deck of the Bridge. He worked his way to the aloft-most bars and floated there, waiting to be spoken to.

Much metal, in many strange shapes, gleamed in the Bridge, and there were irregularly pulsing rainbow surfaces, the closest of which sometimes seemed ranks of files of tiny lights going on and off—red, green, all colors. Aloft of everything was an endless velvet-black expanse very faintly blotched by churning, milky glintings.

Among the metal objects and the rainbows floated figures all clad in the midnight blue of officers. They sometimes gestured to each other, but never spoke a word. To Spar, each of their movements was freighted with profound significance. These were the gods of Windrush, who guided everything, if there were gods at all. He felt reduced in importance to a mouse, which would be chased off chittering if it once broke silence.

After a particularly tense flurry of gestures,

there came a brief distant roar and a familiar creaking and crackling. Spar was amazed, yet at the same time realized he should have known that the Captain, the Navigator, and the rest were responsible for the familiar diurnal phenomena.

It also marked Loafday noon. Spar began to fret. His errands were taking too long. He began to lift his hand tentatively toward each passing figure in midnight blue. None took the least note of him.

Finally he whispered, "Kim—?"

The cat did not reply. He could hear a purring that might be a snore. He gently shook the cat. "Kim, let's talk."

"Shshut offf! I ssleep! Ssh!" Kim resettled himself and his claws and recommenced his purring snore—whether natural or feigned, Spar could not tell. He felt very despondent.

The lunths crept by. He grew desperate and weary. He must not miss his appointment with Doc! He was nerving himself to move farther aloft and speak, when a pleasant, young voice said, "Hello, grandpa, what's on your mind?"

Spar realized that he had been raising his hand automatically and that a person as dark-skinned as Crown, but clad in midnight blue, had at last taken notice. He unzipped the note and handed it over. "For the Exec."

"That's my department." A trilled crackle —fingernail slitting the note? A larger crackle

—note being opened. A brief wait. Then, "Who's Keeper?"

"Owner of the Bat Rack, sir. I work there."

"Bat Rack?"

"A moonbrew mansion. Once called the Happy Torus, I've been told. In the Old Days, Wine Mess Three, Doc told me."

"Hmm. Well, what's all this mean, gramps? And what's your name?"

Spar stared miserably at the dark-mottled gray square. "I can't read, sir. Name's Spar."

"Hmm. Seen any . . . er . . . supernatural beings in the Bat Rack?"

"Only in my dreams, sir."

"Mmm. Well, we'll have a look in. If you recognize me, don't let on. I'm Ensign Drake, by the way. Who's your passenger, grandpa?"

"Only my cat, Ensign," Spar breathed in alarm.

"Well, take the black shaft down." Spar began to move across the monkey jungle in the direction pointed out by the blue armblur.

"And next time remember animals aren't allowed on the Bridge."

As Spar traveled below, his warm relief that Ensign Drake had seemed quite human and compassionate was mixed with anxiety as to whether he still had time to visit Doc. He almost missed the shift to the gang-line grinding aft in the dark red main drag. The corpse-light brightening into the false dawn of late

afternoon bothered him. Once more he passed the tumbling bent figure, this time croaking, "Trinity, Trellis, Wheat Ear . . ."

He was fighting down the urge to give up his visit to Doc and pull home to the Bat Rack, when he noticed he had passed the second squeeze and was in Hold Four with the passageway to Doc's coming up. He dove off, checked himself on a shroud and began the hand-drag to Doc's office, as far larboard as Crown's Hole was starboard.

He passed two figures clumsy on the line, their breaths malty in anticipation of Playday. Spar worried that Doc might have closed his office. He smelled soil and greenery again, from the Gardens of Diana.

The hatch was shut, but when Spar pressed the bulb, it unzipped after three honks, and the white-haloed gray-eyed face peered out.

"I'd just about give up on you, Spar."

"I'm sorry, Doc. I had to—"

"No matter. Come in, come in. Hello, Kim —take a look around if you want."

Kim crawled out, pushed off from Spar's chest, and soon was engaged in a typical cat's tour of inspection.

And there was a great deal to inspect, as even Spar could see. Every shroud in Doc's office seemed to have objects clipped along its entire length. There were blobs large and small, gleaming and dull, light and dark, trans-

lucent and solid. They were silhouetted against a wall of the corpse-light Spar feared, but had no time to think of now. At one end was a band of even brighter light.

"Careful Kim!" Spar called to the cat as he landed against a shroud and began to paw his way from blob to blob.

"He's all right," Doc said. "Let's have a look at you, Spar. Keep your eyes open."

Doc's hands held Spar's head. The gray eyes and leathery face came so close they were one blur.

"Keep them open, I said. Yes, I know you have to blink them, that's all right. Just as I thought. The lenses are dissolved. You've suffered the side-effect which one in ten do who are infected with the Lethean rickettsia."

"Styx ricks, Doc?"

"That's right, though the mob's got hold of the wrong river in the Underworld. But we've all had it. We've all drunk the water of Lethe. Though sometimes when we grow very old we begin to remember the beginning. Don't squirm."

"Hey, Doc, is it because I've had the Styx ricks I can't remember anything back before the Bat Rack?"

"It could be. How long have you been at the Rack?"

"I don't know, Doc. Forever."

"Before I found the place, anyhow. When

the Rumdum closed here in Four. But that's only a starth ago."

"But I'm awful old, Doc. Why don't I start remembering?"

"You're not old, Spar. You're just bald and toothless and etched by moonmist and your muscles have shriveled. Yes, and your mind has shriveled too. Now open your mouth."

One of Doc's hands went to the back of Spar's neck. The other probed. "Your gums are tough, anyhow. That'll make it easier."

Spar wanted to tell about the salt water, but when Doc finally took his hand out of Spar's mouth, it was to say, "Now open wide as you can."

Doc pushed into his mouth something big as a handbag and hot. "Now bite down hard."

Spar felt as if he had bitten fire. He tried to open his mouth, but hands on his head and jaw held it closed. Involuntarily he kicked and clawed air. His eyes filled with tears.

"Stop writhing! Breathe through your nose. It's not that hot. Not hot enough to blister, anyhow."

Spar doubted that, but after a bit decided it wasn't quite hot enough to bake his brain through the roof of his mouth. Besides, he didn't want to show Doc his cowardice. He held still. He blinked several times and the general blur became the blurs of Doc's face and the cluttered room silhouetted by the

corpse-glare. He tried to smile, but his lips were already stretched wider than their muscles could ever have done. That hurt too; he realized now that the heat was abating a little.

Doc was grinning for him. "Well, you would ask an old drunkard to use techniques he'd only read about. To make it up to you, I'll give you teeth sharp enough to sever shrouds. Kim, please get away from that bag."

The black blur of the cat was pushing off from a black blur twice his length. Spar mumbled disapprovingly at Kim through his nose and made motions. The larger blur was shaped like Doc's little bag, but bigger than a hundred of them. It must be massive too, for in reaction to Kim's push it had bent the shroud to which it was attached and—the point—the shroud was very slow in straightening.

"That bag contains my treasure, Spar," Doc explained, and when Spar lifted his eyebrows twice to signal another question, went on, "No, not coin and gold and jewels, but a second transfinite infinitude—sleep and dreams and nightmares for every soul in a thousand Windrushes." He glanced at his wrist. "Time enough now. Open your mouth." Spar obeyed, though it cost him new pain.

Doc withdrew what Spar had bitten on, wrapped it in gleam, and clipped it to the nearest shroud. Then he looked in Spar's mouth again.

"I guess I did make it a bit too hot," he said. He found a small pouch, set it to Spar's lips, and squeezed it. A mist filled Spar's mouth and all pain vanished.

Doc tucked the pouch in Spar's pocket. "If the pain returns, use it again."

But before Spar could thank Doc, the latter had pressed a tube to his eye. "Look, Spar, what do you see?"

Spar cried out, he couldn't help it, and jerked his eye away.

"What's wrong, Spar?"

"Doc, you gave me a dream," Spar said hoarsely. "You won't tell anyone, will you? And it tickled."

"What was the dream like?" Doc asked eagerly.

"Just a picture, Doc. The picture of a goat with the tail of a fish. Doc, I saw the fish's . . ." His mind groped, ". . . scales! Everything had . . . edges! Doc, is *that* what they mean when they talk about seeing sharply?"

"Of course, Spar. This is good. It means there's no cerebral or retinal damage. I'll have no trouble making up field glasses—that is, if there's nothing seriously wrong with my antique pair. So you still see things sharp-edged in dreams—that's natural enough. But why were you afraid of me telling?"

"Afraid of being accused of witchcraft, Doc. I thought seeing things like that was

clairvoyance. The tube tickled my eye a little."

"Isotopes and insanity! It's supposed to tickle. That's the field. Let's try the other eye."

Again Spar wanted to cry out, but he restrained himself, and this time he had no impulse to jerk his eye away, although there was again the faint tickling. The picture was that of a slim girl. He could tell she was female because of her general shape. But he could see her edges. He could see . . . details. For instances, her eyes weren't mist-bounded colored ovals. They had points at both ends, which were china-white . . . triangles. And the pale violet round between the triangles had a tiny black round at its center.

She had silvery hair, yet she looked young, he thought, though it was hard to judge such matters when you could see edges. She made him think of the platinum-haired girl he'd glimpsed in Crown's Hole.

She wore a long, gleaming white dress, which left her shoulders bare, but either art or some unknown force had drawn her hair and her dress toward her feet. In her dress it made . . . folds.

"What's her name, Doc? Almodie?"

"No. Virgo. The Virgin. You can see her edges?"

"Yes, Doc. Sharp. I get it!—like a knife. And the goat-fish?"

"Capricorn," Doc answered, removing the tube from Spar's eye.

"Doc, I know Capricorn and Virgo are the names of lunths, terranths, sunths, and starths, but I never knew they had pictures. I never knew they *were* anything."

"You— Of course, you've never seen watches, or stars, let alone the constellations of the zodiac."

Spar was about to ask what all *those* were, but then he saw that the corpse-light was all gone, although the ribbon of brighter light had grown very wide.

"At least in this stretch of your memory," Doc added. "I should have your new eyes and teeth ready next Loafday. Come earlier if you can manage. I may see you before that at the Bat Rack, Playday night or earlier."

"Great, Doc, but now I've got to haul. Come on, Kim! Sometimes business heavies up Loafday night, Doc, like it was Playday night come at the wrong end. Jump in, Kim."

"Sure you can make it back to the Bat Rack all right, Spar? It'll be dark before you get there."

"Course I can, Doc."

But when night fell, like a heavy hood jerked down over his head, halfway down the first passageway, he would have gone back to ask Doc to guide him, except he feared Kim's contempt, even though the cat still wasn't

talking. He pulled ahead rapidly, though the few running lights hardly let him see the centerline.

The fore gangway was even worse—completely empty and its lights dim and flickering. Seeing by blurs bothered him now that he knew what seeing sharp was like. He was beginning to sweat and shake and cramp from his withdrawal from alcohol and his thoughts were a tumult. He wondered if *any* of the weird things that had happened since meeting Kim were real or dream. Kim's refusal—or inability?—to talk any more was disquieting. He began seeing the misty rims of blurs that vanished when he looked straight toward them. He remembered Keeper and the brewos talking about vamps and witches.

Then instead of waiting for the Bat Rack's green hatch, he dove off into the passageway leading to the aft one. This passageway had no lights at all. Out of it he thought he could hear Hellhound growling, but couldn't be sure because the big chewer was grinding. He was scrabbling with panic when he entered the Bat Rack through the dark red hatch, remembering barely in time to avoid the new glue.

The place was jumping with light and excitement and dancing figures, and Keeper at once began to shout abuse at him. He dove into the torus and began taking orders and serving automatically, working entirely by

touch and voice, because withdrawal now had his vision swimming—a spinning blur of blurs.

After a while that got better, but his nerves got worse. Only the unceasing work kept him going—and shut out Keeper's abuse—but he was getting too tired to work at all. As Playday dawned, with the crowd around the torus getting thicker all the while, he snatched a pouch of moonmist and set it to his lips.

Claws dug his chest. "Isssiot! Sssot! Ssslave of fffear!"

Spar almost went into convulsions, but put back the moonmist. Kim came out of the slopsuit and pushed off contemptuously, circled the bar and talked to various of the drinkers, soon became a conversation piece. Keeper started to boast about him and quit serving. Spar worked on and on and on through sobriety more nightmarish than any drunk he could recall. And far, far longer.

Suzy came in with a mark and touched Spar's hand when he served her dark to her. It helped.

He thought he recognized a voice from below. It came from a kinky-haired, slopsuited brewo he didn't know. But then he heard the man again and thought he was Ensign Drake. There were several brewos he didn't recognize.

The place started really jumping. Keeper

upped the music. Singly or in pairs, somer-saulting dancers bounded back and forth between shrouds. Others toed a shroud and shimmied. A girl in black did splits on one. A girl in white dove through the torus. Keeper put it on her boyfriend's check. Brewos tried to sing.

Spar heard Kim recite:

"Izz a cat.

Killzz a rat.

Greetss each guy.

Thin or ffat.

Saay dolls, hi!"

Playday night fell. The place got hotter. Doc didn't come. But Crown did. Dancers parted and a whole section of drinkers made way aloft for him and his girls and Hellhound, so that they had a third of the torus to themselves, with no one below in that third either. To Spar's surprise they all took coffee except the dog, who when asked by Crown, responded, "Bloody Mary," drawing out the words in such deep tones that they were little more than a low "Bluh-Muh" growl.

"Iss that sspeech, I assk you?" Kim commented from the other side of the torus. Drunks around him choked down chuckles.

Spar served the pouched coffee piping hot with felt holders and mixed Hellhound's drink in a self-squeezing syringe with sipping tube. He was very groggy and for the moment more

afraid for Kim than himself. The face blurs tended to swim, but he could distinguish Rixende by her black hair, Phanette and Doucette by their matching red-blonde hair and oddly red-mottled fair skins, while Almodie *was* the platinum-haired pale one, yet she looked horribly right between the dark brown, purple-vested blur to one side of her and the blacked, narrower, prick-eared silhouette to the other.

Spar heard Crown whisper to her, "Ask Keeper to show you the talking cat." The whisper was very low and Spar wouldn't have heard it except that Crown's voice had a strange excited vibrancy Spar had never known in it before.

"But won't they fight then?—I mean Hellhound," she answered in a voice that sent silvery tendrils around Spar's heart. He yearned to see her face through Doc's tube. She would look like Virgo, only more beautiful. Yet, Crown's girl, she could be no virgin. It was a strange and horrible world. Her eyes *were* violet. But he was sick of blurs. Almodie sounded very frightened, yet she continued, "Please don't, Crown." Spar's heart was captured.

"But that's the whole idea, baby. And nobody dont's us. We thought we'd schooled you to that. We'd teach you another lesson here, except tonight we smell high fuzz—lots of it,

Keeper!—our new lady wishes to hear your cat talk. Bring it over."

"I really don't . . ." Almodie began and went no further.

Kim came floating across the torus while Keeper was shouting in the opposite direction. The cat checked himself against a slender shroud and looked straight at Crown. "Yesss?"

"Keeper, shut that junk off." The music died abruptly. Voices rose, then died abruptly too. "Well, cat, talk."

"Shshall ssing insstead," Kim announced and began an eerie caterwauling that had a pattern but was not Spar's idea of music.

"It's an abstraction," Almodie breathed delightedly. "Listen, Crown, that was a diminished seventh."

"A demented third, I'd say," Phanette commented from the other side.

Crown signed them to be quiet.

Kim finished with a high trill. He slowly looked around at his baffled audience and then began to groom his shoulder.

Crown gripped a ridge of the torus with his left hand and said evenly, "Since you will not talk to us, will you talk to our dog?"

Kim stared at Hellhound sucking his Bloody Mary. His eyes widened, their pupils slitted, his lips writhed back from needle-like fangs.

He hissed, "Schschweinhund!"

Hellhound launched himself, hind paws

against the palm of Crown's left hand, which threw him forward toward the left, where Kim was dodging. But the cat switched directions, rebounding hindwards from the next shroud. The dog's white-jagged jaws snapped sideways a foot from their mark as his great-chested black body hurtled past.

Hellhound landed with four paws in the middle of a fat drunk, who puffed out his wind barely before his swallow, but the dog took off instantly on reverse course. Kim bounced back and forth between shrouds. This time hair flew when jaws snapped, but also a rigidly spread paw slashed.

Crown grabbed Hellhound by his studded collar, restraining him from another dive. He touched the dog below the eye and smelled his fingers. "That'll be enough, boy," he said. "Can't go around killing musical geniuses." His hand dropped from his nose to below the torus and came up loosely fisted. "Well, cat, you've talked with our dog. Have you a word for us?"

"Yesss!" Kim drifted to the shroud nearest Crown's face. Spar pushed off to grab him back, while Almodie gazed at Crown's fist and edged a hand toward it.

Kim loudly hissed, "Hellzzz ssspawn! Fffiend!"

Both Spar and Almodie were too late. From between two of Crown's fisted fingers a

needle-stream jetted and struck Kim in the open mouth.

After what seemed to Spar a long time, his hand interrupted the stream. Its back burned acutely.

Kim seemed to collapse into himself, then launched himself away from Crown, toward the dark, open-jawed.

Crown said, "That's mace, an antique weapon like Greek fire, but well-known to our folk. The perfect answer to a witch cat."

Spar sprang at Crown, grappled his chest, tried to butt his jaw. They moved away from the torus at half the speed with which Spar had sprung.

Crown got his head aside. Spar closed his gums on Crown's throat. There was a *snick*. Spar felt wind on his bare back. Then a cold triangle pressed his flesh over his kidneys. Spar opened his jaws and floated limp. Crown chuckled.

A blue fuzz-glare, held by a brewo, made everyone in the Bat Rack look more corpse-like than larboard light. A voice commanded, "Okay, folks, break it up. Go home. We're closing the place."

Sleepday dawned, drowning the fuzz-glare. The cold triangle left Spar's back. There was another *snick*. Saying, "Bye-bye, baby," Crown pushed off through the white glare toward four women's faces and one dog's.

Phanette's and Doucette's faintly red-mottled ones were close beside Hellhound's, as if they might be holding his collar.

Spar sobbed and began to hunt for Kim. After a while Suzy came to help him. The Bat Rack emptied. Spar and Suzy cornered Kim. Spar grasped the cat around the chest. Kim's forelegs embraced his wrist, claws pricking. Spar got out the pouch Doc had given him and shoved its mouth between Kim's jaws. The claws dug deep. Taking no note of that, Spar gently sprayed. Gradually the claws came out and Kim relaxed. Spar hugged him gently. Suzy bound up Spar's wounded wrist.

Keeper came up followed by two brewos, one of them Ensign Drake, who said, "My partner and I will watch today by the aft and starboard hatches." Beyond them the Bat Rack was empty.

Spar said, "Crown has a knife." Drake nodded.

Suzy touched Spar's hand and said, "Keeper, I want to stay here tonight. I'm scared."

Keeper said, "I can offer you a shroud."

Drake and his mate dove slowly toward their posts.

Suzy squeezed Spar's hand. He said, rather heavily, "I can offer you my shroud, Suzy."

Keeper laughed and after looking toward the Bridge men, whispered, "I can offer you mine, which, unlike Spar, I own. And moonmist. Otherwise, the passageways."

Suzy sighed, paused, then went off with him.

Spar miserably made his way to the fore corner. Had Suzy expected him to fight Keeper? The sad thing was that he no longer wanted her, except as a friend. He loved Crown's new girl. Which was sad too.

He was very tired. Even the thought of new eyes tomorrow didn't interest him. He clipped his ankle to a shroud and tied a rag over his eyes. He gently clasped Kim, who had not spoken. He was asleep at once.

He dreamed of Almodie. She looked like Virgo, even to the white dress. She held Kim, who looked sleek as polished black leather. She was coming toward him smiling. She kept coming without getting closer.

Much later—he thought—he woke in the grip of withdrawal. He sweated and shook, but those were minor. His nerves were jumping. Any moment, he was sure, they would twitch all his muscles into a stabbing spasm of sinew-snapping agony. His thoughts were moving so fast he could hardly begin to understand one in ten. It was like speeding through a curving, ill-lit passageway ten times faster than the main drag. If he touched a wall, he would forget even what little Spar knew, forget he was Spar. All around him black shrouds whipped in perpetual sine curves.

Kim was no longer by him. He tore the rag from his eyes. It was dark as before. Sleepday

57

night. But his body stopped speeding and his thoughts slowed. His nerves still crackled, and he still saw the black snakes whipping, but he knew them for illusion. He even made out the dim glows of three running lights.

Then he saw two figures floating toward him. He could barely make out their eye-blurs, green in the smaller, violet in the other, whose face was spreadingly haloed by silvery glints. She was pale and whiteness floated around her. And instead of a smile, he could see the white horizontal blur of bared teeth. Kim's teeth too were bared.

Suddenly he remembered the golden-haired girl who he'd thought was playing bartender in Crown's Hole. She was Suzy's one-time friend Sweetheart, snatched last Sleepday by vamps.

He screamed, which in Spar was a hoarse, retching bellow, and scrabbled at his clipped ankle.

The figures vanished. Below, he thought.

Lights came on. Someone dove and shook Spar's shoulder. "What happened, gramps?"

Spar gibbered while he thought what to tell Drake. He loved Almodie and Kim. He said, "Had a nightmare. Vamps attacked me."

"Description?"

"An old lady and a . . . a . . . little dog."

The other officer dove in. "The black hatch is open."

58

Drake said, "Keeper told us that was always locked. Follow through, Fenner." As the other dove below, "You're sure this was a nightmare, gramps? A *little* dog? And an *old* woman?"

Spar said, "Yes," and Drake dove after his comrade, out through the black hatch.

Workday dawned. Spar felt sick and confused, but he set about his usual routine. He tried to talk to Kim, but the cat was as silent as yesterday afternoon. Keeper bullied and found many tasks—the place was a mess from Playday. Suzy got away quickly. She didn't want to talk about Sweetheart or anything else. Drake and Fenner didn't come back.

Spar swept and Kim patrolled, out of touch. In the afternoon Crown came in and talked with Keeper while Spar and Kim were out of earshot. They mightn't have been there for all notice Crown took of them.

Spar wondered about what he had seen last night. It might really have been a dream, he decided. He was no longer impressed by his memory-identification of Sweetheart. Stupid of him to have thought that Almodie and Kim, dream or reality, were vamps. Doc had said vamps were superstitions. But he didn't think much. He still had withdrawal symptoms, only less violent.

When Loafday dawned, Keeper gave Spar permission to leave the Bat Rack without his usual prying questions. Spar looked around for

Kim, but couldn't see his black blob. Besides, he didn't really want to take the cat.

He went straight to Doc's office. The passageways weren't as lonely as last Loafday. For a third time he passed the bent figure croaking, "Seagull, Kestrel, Cathedral . . ."

Doc's hatch was unzipped, but Doc wasn't there. Kim waited a long while, uneasy in the corpse-light. It wasn't like Doc to leave his office unzipped and unattended. And he hadn't turned up at the Bat Rack last night, as he'd half promised.

Finally Spar began to look around. One of the first things he noticed was that the big black bag, which Doc had said contained his treasure, was missing.

Then he noticed that the gleaming pliofilm bag in which Doc had put the mold of Spar's gums, now held something different. He unclipped it from its shroud. There were two items in it.

He cut a finger on the first, which was half circle, half pink and half gleaming. He felt out its shape more cautiously then, ignoring the tiny red blobs welling from his finger. It had irregular depressions in its pink top and bottom. He put it in his mouth. His gums mated with the depressions. He opened his mouth; then closed it, careful to keep his tongue back. There was a *snick* and a dull *click*. He had teeth!

His hands were shaking, not just from withdrawal, as he felt the second item.

It was two thick rounds joined by a short bar and with a thicker long bar ending in a semicircle going back from each.

He thrust a finger into one of the rounds. It tickled, just as the tube had tickled his eyes, only more intensely, almost painfully.

Hands shaking worse than ever, he fitted the contraption to his face. The semicircles went around his ears, the rounds circled his eyes, not closely enough to tickle.

He could see sharply! *Everything* had edges, even his spread-fingered hands and the . . . clot of blood on one finger. He cried out—a low, wondering wail—and scanned the office. At first the scores and dozens of sharp-edged objects, each as distinct as the pictures of Capricorn and Virgo had been, were too much for him. He closed his eyes.

When his breathing was a little evener and his shaking less, he opened them cautiously and began to inspect the objects clipped to the shrouds. Each one was a wonder. He didn't know the purpose of half of them. Some of them with which he was familiar by use or blurred sight startled him greatly in their appearance—a comb, a brush, a book with pages (that infinitude of ranked black marks), a wrist watch (the tiny pictures around the circular margin of Capricorn and Virgo, and of

the Bull and the Fishes, and so on, and the narrow bars radiating from the center and swinging swiftly or slowly or not at all—and pointing to the signs of the zodiac).

Before he knew it, he was at the corpse-glow wall. He faced it with a new courage, though it forced from his lips another wondering wail.

The corpse-glow didn't come from everywhere, though it took up the central quarter of his field of vision. His fingers touched taut, transparent pliofilm. What he saw beyond—a great way beyond, he began to think—was utter blackness with a great many tiny . . . points of bright light in it. Points were even harder to believe in than edges, but he had to believe what he saw.

But centrally, looking much bigger than all the blackness, was a vast corpse-white round pocked with faint circles and scored by bright lines and mottled with slightly darker areas.

It didn't look as if it were wired for electricity, and it certainly didn't look afire. After a while Spar got the weird idea that its light was reflected from something much brighter *behind* Windrush. ·

It was infinitely strange to think of so much *space* around Windrush. Like thinking of a reality containing reality.

And if Windrush were between the hypothetical brighter light and the pocked white round, its shadow ought to be on the latter.

Unless Windrush were almost infinitely small. Really these speculations were utterly too fantastic to deal with.

Yet could anything be too fantastic? Werewolves, witches, points, edges, size and space beyond any but the most insane belief.

When he had first looked at the corpsewhite object, it had been round. And he had heard and felt the creakings of Loafday noon, without being conscious of it at the time. But now the round had its fore edge evenly sliced off, so that it was lopsided. Spar wondered if the hypothetical incandescence behind Windrush were moving, or the white round rotating, or Windrush itself revolving around the white round. Such thoughts, especially the last, were dizzying almost beyond endurance.

He made for the open door, wondering if he should zip it behind him, decided not to. The passageway was another amazement, going off and off and off, and narrowing as it went. Its walls bore . . . arrows, the red pointing to larboard, the way from which he'd come, the green pointing starboard, the way he was going. The arrows were what he'd always seen as dash-shaped blurs. As he pulled himself along the strangely definite drag-line, the passageway stayed the same diameter, all the way to the violet main-drag.

He wanted to jerk himself as fast as the green arrows to the starboard end of

Windrush to verify the hypothetical incandescence and see the details of the orange-dun round that always depressed him.

But he decided he ought first to report Doc's disappearance to the Bridge. He might find Drake there. And report the loss of Doc's treasure too, he reminded himself.

Passing faces fascinated him. Such a welter of noses and ears! He overtook the croaking, bent shape. It was that of an old woman whose nose almost met her chin. She was doing something twitchy with her fingers to two narrow sticks and a roll of slender, fuzzy line. He impulsively dove off the drag-line and caught hold of her, whirling them around.

"What are you doing, grandma?" he asked.

She puffed with anger. "Knitting," she answered indignantly.

"What are the words you keep saying?"

"Names of knitting patterns," she replied, jerking loose from him and blowing on. "Sand Dunes, Lightning, Soldiers Marching . . ."

He started to swim for the drag-line, then saw he was already at the blue shaft leading aloft. He grabbed hold of its speeding centerline, not minding the burn, and speeded to the Bridge.

When he got there, he saw there was a multitude of stars aloft. The oblong rainbows were all banks of multi-colored lights winking on and off. But the silent officers—they looked very old, their faces stared as if they

were sleep-swimming, their gestured orders were mechanical, he wondered if they knew where Windrush was going—or anything at all, beyond the Bridge of Windrush.

A dark, young officer with tightly curly hair floated to him. It wasn't until he spoke that Spar knew he was Ensign Drake.

"Hello, gramps. Say, you look younger. What are those things around your eyes?"

"Field glasses. They help me see sharp."

"But field glasses have tubes. They're a sort of binocular telescope."

Spar shrugged and told about the disappearance of Doc and his big, black treasure bag.

"But you say he drank a lot and he told you his treasures were dreams? Sounds like he was wacky and wandered off to do his drinking somewhere else."

"But Doc was a regular drinker. He always came to the Bat Rack."

"Well, I'll do what I can. Say, I've been pulled off the Bat Rack investigation. I think that character Crown got at someone higher up. The old ones are easy to get at—not so much greed as going by custom, taking the easiest course. Fenner and I never did find the old woman and the little dog, or any female and animal . . . or anything."

Spar told about Crown's earlier attempt to steal Doc's little black bag.

"So you think the two cases might be connected. Well, as I say, I'll do what I can."

Spar went back to the Bat Rack. It was very strange to see Keeper's face in detail. It looked old and its pink target center was a big red nose criss-crossed by veins. His brown eyes were not so much curious as avid. He asked about the things around Spar's eyes. Spar decided it wouldn't be wise to tell Keeper about seeing sharply.

"They're a new kind of costume jewelry, Keeper. Blasted Earth, I don't have any hair on my head, ought to have something.

"Language, Spar! It's like a drunk to spend precious scrip on such a grotesque bauble."

Spar neither reminded Keeper that all the scrip he'd earned at the Bat Rack amounted to no more than a wad as big as his thumb-joint, nor that he'd quit drinking. Nor did he tell him about his teeth, but kept them hidden behind his lips.

Kim was nowhere in sight. Keeper shrugged. "Gone off somewhere. You know the way of strays, Spar."

Yes, thought Spar, this one's stayed put too long.

He kept being amazed that he could see *all* of the Bat Rack sharply. It was an octahedron criss-crossed by shrouds and made up of two pyramids put together square base to square base. The apexes of the pyramids were the violet fore and dark red aft corners. The four other corners were the starboard green, the black below, the larboard scarlet, and the blue

aloft, if you named them from aft in the way the hands of a watch move.

Suzy drifted in early Playday. Spar was shocked by her blowzy appearance and blood-shot eyes. But he was touched by her signs of affection and he felt the strong friendship between them. Twice when Keeper wasn't looking he switched her nearly empty pouch of dark for a full one. She told him that, yes, she'd once known Sweetheart and that, yes, she'd heard people say Mabel had seen Sweetheart snatched by vamps.

Business was slow for Playday. There were no strange brewos. Hoping against fearful, gut-level certainty, Spar kept waiting for Doc to come in zig-zagging along the ratlines and comment on the new gadgets he'd given Spar and spout about the Old Days and his strange philosophy.

Playday night Crown came in with his girls, all except Almodie. Doucette said she'd had a headache and stayed at the Hole. Once again, all of them ordered coffee, though to Spar all of them seemed high.

Spar covertly studied their faces. Though nervous and alive, they all had something in their stares akin to those he'd seen in most of the officers on the Bridge. Doc had said they were all zombies. It was interesting to find out that Phanette's and Doucette's red-mottled appearance was due to . . . freckles, tiny red-dish star-clusters on their white skins.

"Where's that famous talking cat?" Crown asked Spar.

Spar shrugged. Keeper said, "Strayed. For which I'm glad. Don't want a little feline who makes fights like last night."

Keeping his yellow-brown irised eyes on Spar, Crown said, "We believe it was that fight last Playday gave Almodie her headache, so she didn't want to come back tonight. We'll tell her you got rid of the witch cat."

"I'd have got rid of the beast if Spar hadn't," Keeper put in. "So you think it was a witch cat, coroner?"

"We're certain. What's that stuff on Spar's face?"

"A new sort of cheap eye-jewelry, coroner, such as attracts drunks."

Spar got the feeling that this conversation had been prearranged, that there was a new agreement between Crown and Keeper. But he just shrugged again. Suzy was looking angry, but she said nothing.

Yet she stayed behind again after the Bat Rack closed. Keeper put no claim on her, though he leered knowingly before disappearing with a yawn and a stretch through the scarlet hatch. Spar checked that all six hatches were locked and shut off the lights, though that made no difference in the morning glare, before returning to Suzy, who had gone to his sleeping shroud.

Suzy asked, "You didn't get rid of Kim?"

Spar answered, "No, he just strayed, as Keeper said at first. I don't know where Kim is."

Suzy smiled and put her arms around him. "I think your new eye-things are beautiful," she said.

Spar said, "Suzy, did you know that Windrush isn't the Universe? That's it's a ship going through space around a white round marked with circles, a round much bigger than all Windrush?"

Suzy replied, "I know Windrush is sometimes called the Ship. I've seen that round—in pictures. Forget all wild thoughts, Spar, and lose yourself in me."

Spar did so, chiefly from friendship. He forgot to clip his ankle to the shroud. Suzy's body didn't attract him. He was thinking of Almodie.

When it was over, Suzy slept. Spar put the rag around his eyes and tried to do the same. He was troubled by withdrawal symptoms only a little less bad than last Sleepday's. Because of that little, he didn't go to the torus for a pouch of moonmist. But then there was a sharp jab in his back, as if a muscle had spasmed there, and the symptoms got much worse. He convulsed, once, twice, then just as the agony became unbearable, blanked out.

Spar woke, his head throbbing, to discover

that he was not only clipped, but lashed to his shroud, his wrists stretched in one direction, his ankles in the other, his hands and his feet both numb. His nose rubbed the shroud.

Light made his eyelids red. He opened them a little at a time and saw Hellhound poised with bent hind legs against the next shroud. He could see Hellhound's great stabbing teeth very clearly. If he had opened his eyes a little more swiftly, Hellhound would have dived at his throat.

He rubbed his sharp metal teeth together. At least he had more than gums to meet an attack on his face.

Beyond Hellhound he saw black and transparent spirals. He realized he was in Crown's Hole. Evidently the last jab in his back had been the injection of a drug.

But Crown had not taken away his eye jewelry, nor noted his teeth. He had thought of Spar as old Eyeless Toothless.

Between Hellhound and the spirals, he saw Doc lashed to a shroud and his big black bag clipped next to him. Doc was gagged. Evidently he had tried to cry out. Spar decided not to. Doc's gray eyes were open and Spar thought Doc was looking at him.

Very slowly Spar moved his numb fingers on top of the knot lashing his wrists to the shroud and slowly contracted all his muscles and pulled. The knot slid down the shroud a millimeter. So long as he did something slowly

enough, Hellhound could not see it. He repeated this action at intervals.

Even more slowly he swung his face to the left. He saw nothing more than that the hatch to the corridor was zipped shut, and that beyond the dog and Doc, between the black spirals, was an empty and unfurnished cabin whose whole starboard side was stars. The hatch to that cabin was open, with its black-striped emergency hatch wavering beside it.

With equal slowness he swung his face to the right, past Doc and past Hellhound, who was eagerly watching him for signs of life or waking. He had pulled down the knot on his wrists two centimeters.

The first thing he saw was a transparent oblong. In it were more stars and, by its aft edge, the smoky orange round. At last he could see the latter more clearly. The smoke was on top, the orange underneath and irregularly placed. The whole was about as big as Spar's palm could have covered, if he had been able to stretch out his arm to full length. As he watched, he saw a bright flash in one of the orange areas. The flash was short, then it turned to a tiny black round pushing out through the smoke. More than ever, Spar felt sadness.

Below the transparency, Spar saw a horrible tableau. Suzy was strapped to a bright metal rack guyed by shrouds. She was very pale and her eyes were closed. From the side of her

neck went a red sipping-tube which forked into five branches. Four of the branches went into the red mouths of Crown, Rixende, Phanette, and Doucette. The fifth was shut by a small metal clip, and beyond it Almodie floated cowering, hands over her eyes.

Crown said softly, "We want it all. Strip her, Rixie."

Rixende clipped shut the end of her tube and swam to Suzy. Spar expected her to remove the blue culottes and bra, but instead she simply began to massage one of Suzy's legs, pressing always from ankle toward waist, driving her remaining blood nearer her neck.

Crown removed his sipping tube from his lips long enough to say, "Ahhh, good to the last drop." Then he had mouthed the blood that had spurted out in the interval and had the tube in place again.

Phanette and Doucette convulsed with soundless giggles.

Almodie peered between her parted fingers, out of her mass of platinum hair, then scissored them shut again.

After a while Crown said, "That's all we'll get. Phan and Doucie, feed her to the big chewer. If you meet anyone in the passageway, pretend she's drunk. Afterwards we'll get Doc to dose us high, and give him a little brew if he behaves, then we'll drink Spar."

Spar had his wrist knot more than halfway to

his teeth. Hellhound kept watching eagerly for movement, unable to see movement that slow. Slaver made tiny gray globes beside his fangs.

Phanette and Doucette opened the hatch and steered Suzy's dead body through it.

Embracing Rixende, Crown said expansively toward Doc, "Well, isn't it the right thing, old man? Nature bloody in tooth and claw, a wise one said. They've poisoned everything there." He pointed toward the smoky orange round sliding out of sight. "They're still fighting, but they'll soon all be dead. So death should be the rule too for this gimcrack, so-called survival ship. Remember they are aboard her. When we've drunk the blood of everyone aboard Windrush, including their blood, we'll drink our own, if our own isn't theirs."

Spar thought, Crown thinks too much in they's. The knot was close to his teeth. He heard the big chewer start to grind.

In the empty next cabin, Spar saw Drake and Fenner, clad once more as brewos, swimming toward the open hatch.

But Crown saw them too. "Get 'em, Hellhound," he directed, pointing. "It's our command."

The big black dog bulleted from his shroud through the open hatch. Drake pointed something at him. The dog went limp.

Chuckling softly, Crown took by one tip a swastika with curved, gleaming, razor-sharp

blades and sent it off spinning. It curved past Spar and Doc, went through the open hatch, missed Drake and Fenner—and Hellhound—and struck the wall of stars.

There was a rush of wind, then the emergency hatch smacked shut. Spar saw Drake, Fenner and Hellhound, wavery through the transparent pliofilm, spew blood, bloat, burst bloodily open. The empty cabin they had been in disappeared. Windrush had a new wall and Crown's Hole was distorted.

Far beyond, growing even tinier, the swastika spun toward the stars.

Phanette and Doucette came back. "We buried Suzy. Someone was coming, so we beat it." The big chewer stopped grinding.

Spar bit cleanly through his wrist lashings and immediately doubled over to bite his ankles loose.

Crown dove at him. Pausing to draw knives, the four girls did the same.

Phanette, Doucette, and Rixende went limp. Spar had the impression that small black balls had glanced from their skulls.

There wasn't time to bite his feet loose, so he straightened. Crown hit his chest as Almodie hit his feet.

Crown and Spar giant-swung around the shroud. Then Almodie had cut Spar's ankles loose. As they spun off along the tangent, Spar tried to knee Crown in the groin, but Crown

twisted and evaded the blow as they moved toward the inboard wall.

There was the *snick* of Crown's knife unfolding. Spar saw the dark wrist and grabbed it. He butted at Crown's jaw. Crown evaded. Spar set his teeth in Crown's neck and bit.

Blood covered Spar's face, spurted over it. He spat out a hunk of flesh. Crown convulsed. Spar fought off the knife. Crown went limp. That the pressure in a man should work against him.

Spar shook the blood from his face. Through its beads, he saw Keeper and Kim side by side. Almodie was clutching his ankles. Phanette, Doucette, Rixende floated.

Keeper said proudly, "I shot them with my gun for drunks. I knocked them out. Now I'll cut their throats, if you wish."

Spar said, "No more throat-cutting. No more blood." Shaking off Almodie's hands, he took off for Doc, picking up Doucette's floating knife by the way.

He slashed Doc's lashings and cut the gag from his face.

Meanwhile Kim hissed, "Sstole and ssecreted Keeper's sscrip from the boxx. Ashshured him you sstole it, Sspar. You and Ssuzzy. Sso he came. Keeper izz a shshlemiel."

Keeper said, "I saw Suzy's foot going into the big chewer. I knew it by its anklet of

hearts. After that I had the courage to kill Crown or anyone. I loved Suzy."

Doc cleared his throat and croaked, "Moonmist." Spar found a triple pouch and Doc sucked it all. Doc said, "Crown spoke the truth. Windrush is a plastic survival ship from Earth. Earth—" He motioned toward the dull orange round disappearing aft in the window "—poisoned herself with smog pollution and with nuclear war. She spent gold for war, plastic for survival. Best forgotten. Windrush went mad. Understandably. Even without the Lethean rickettsia, or Styx ricks, as you call it. Thought Windrush was the cosmos. Crown kidnapped me to get my drugs, kept me alive to know the doses."

Spar looked at Keeper. "Clean up here," he ordered. "Feed Crown to the big chewer."

Almodie pulled herself from Spar's ankles to his waist. "There was a second survival ship. Circumluna. When Windrush went mad, my father and mother—and you—were sent here, to investigate and cure. But my father died and you got Styx ricks. My mother died just before I was given to Crown. She sent you Kim."

Kim hissed, "My fforebear came from Circumluna to Windrush, too. Great grandmother. Taught me the ffigures for Windrushsh . . . Radiuss from moon-ccenter, 2,500 miles. Period, ssixx hours—sso, the sshort dayss. A terranth izz the time it takess

Earth to move through a consstellation, and sso on."

Doc said, "So, Spar, you're the only one who remembers without cynicism. You'll have to take over. It's all yours, Spar."

Spar had to agree.